GROUND
WORKS

ALSO BY CHRISTIAN BÖK

POETRY
Eunoia
Crystallography

CRITICISM
'Pataphysics: The Poetics of an Imaginary Science

GROUND WORKS

AVANT-GARDE
FOR THEE

EDITED BY
CHRISTIAN BÖK
INTRODUCTION BY
MARGARET ATWOOD

ANANSI

Published in 2002 by
House of Anansi Press Inc.
110 Spadina Avenue, Suite 801
Toronto, ON, M5V 2K4
Tel. 416-363-4343
Fax 416-363-1017
www.anansi.ca

Distributed in Canada by
Publishers Group Canada
250A Carlton Street
Toronto, ON, M5A 2L1
Tel. 416-934-9900
Toll free order numbers:
Tel. 800-663-5714
Fax 800-565-3770

06 05 04 03 02   1 2 3 4 5

NATIONAL LIBRARY OF CANADA CATALOGUING IN PUBLICATION DATA

Main entry under title:
Ground works : Avant-garde for thee

ISBN 0-88784-180-5

1. Experimental fiction, Canadian (English)
2. Canadian fiction (English)—20th century. I. Bök, Christian, 1966–

PS8329.G76 2002   C813'.5408011   C2002-900330-X
PR9197.3.G76 2002

Jacket and text design: Bill Douglas @ The Bang
Text layout: Tannice Goddard

THE CANADA COUNCIL | LE CONSEIL DES ARTS
FOR THE ARTS | DU CANADA
SINCE 1957 | DEPUIS 1957

*We acknowledge for their financial support of our publishing
program the Canada Council for the Arts, the Ontario Arts Council,
and the Government of Canada through the Book Publishing
Industry Development Program (BPIDP).*

Printed and bound in Canada

CONTENTS

CONTENTS CONTINUED

GROUND
WORKS

INTRODUCTION
BY MARGARET ATWOOD

GROUND WORKS is an anthology of experimental fiction by writers who emerged on the wilder shores of literature in this country almost forty years ago.

I admit to being the instigator of this book. I agitated for it because a body of work that deserved to be recalled and set within its original frame was slipping from view, leaving the young with the impression that there was nothing unorthodox in this country before folks started getting their tongues pierced. But I did not want to trust my own now somewhat arthritic judgement, so Christian Bök, a young experimental writer of the twenty-first century, was asked to do the selecting and arranging, and is thus the book's primary editor. The result is a sort of Ogopogo Creature: you've heard the rumours about an invisible, impossible weirdness, now here's the blurry snapshot. See? There was something down there all along!

The term "experimental fiction" covers a lot of territory. It also makes me a little nervous, as I grew up with scientists and know their single-minded ways, and the term itself is a tribute to the early twentieth century's reverence for that particular branch of human knowledge. The reverence may have faded somewhat, but the term remains, leaving behind a faint whiff of formaldehyde and Dr. Frankenstein: the dissection of language and narrative, and their reassembly into talking monsters, can strike us as cold-blooded. Dr. Frankenstein himself was not cold-blooded, however; he was a disrupter of social norms, a breaker of laws, a subversive idealist, a feverish believer in the new and the potential; and so it is with many "experimental" writers.

In what ways can fiction be "experimental"? On the one hand, all fiction is experimental, in that it ventures into the unknown and attempts to prove a hypothesis. Thus:

Hypothesis: a) That this piece of fiction can actually be written by the author attempting it, and b) that it can thereafter hold a reader's attention.

Demonstration: The piece of fiction.

Conclusion: Someone actually reads the book all the way through, without throwing it against the wall.

But that's too broad. What we usually mean by "experimental fiction" is fiction that sets up certain rules for itself — rules that are not the same as those followed by the mainstream fiction of its day — and then proceeds to obey its own new commandments, while subverting the conventions according to which readers have understood what constitutes a proper work of literature. There's a faint air of peeking beneath the skirts, of snooping behind the rhetorical scenes. Pieces like these can border on the parody or the extended joke — Woody Allen's story about the machine that allows real people to get into well-known books as characters, Pozzo's send-up rendition of a sunset description in *Waiting for Godot*, Michael Ondaatje's use of pulp romance conventions to syncopate his Billy the Kid saga — which does not exclude the possibility of their being at the same time deeply unsettling. Accepted narrative lines are turned upside down, language is stretched and pulled inside out, characters don't remain "within character." Thus the writers in this anthology — at least in the work represented here — were more interested in colouring outside the lines than within them, and some even had it in mind to toss the entire colouring book into the fire and start with a whole new sheet of paper.

What was it that made the Canada of the 60s such fertile ground for this kind of writing? Partly it was a stranger place in many ways than is often supposed — who remembers the LSD that flowed so freely in London, Ontario, in the 1950s — well before the age of Timothy Leary — not to mention the orgies in the cathedral? It was strange in a literary way as well. What other country would have produced a set of Spenserian eclogues spoken in a farmyard by a flock of geese? (*A Suit of Nettles*, James Reaney, 1958.) Partly, also, it was an open field — some might say a vacant lot. Many of the conditions taken for granted today — that there is a Canadian "canon," that a Canadian writer can be widely known, respected, and solvent, that you can get a grant or a film contract or teach creative writing or win big prizes, that there are such things as book-promotion tours and literary festivals, that it is possible to live in Canada and function as a professional writer with a national, indeed an international "career" — these conditions scarcely existed in the writing world of the 50s and 60s, when the writers collected here had their toes on the starting line. Nature abhors a vacuum, and so does literature. There is nothing more conducive to scribbling than a blank page.

There had been well-known Canadian fiction writers earlier — L. M. Montgomery of *Anne of Green Gables* fame, for instance, or Mazo De La Roche of the Jalna books, or, on higher literary ground, Morley Callaghan — but as a rule these had entered the scene through non-Canadian publishers, and were then distributed in Canada through agents or branch plants. There was, too, a Canadian-owned publishing industry, which even had a cheap-hardback mass-distribution side to it, but the Depression, the Second World War, and the advent of the U.S.-controlled paperback industry had kicked large holes in that. After the war, the old order changed: the British Empire as a political force was all but defunct, and any writer associated with it was passé; the new wave of money coming into Canada was American, as was the new wave of widely-read writers. This was — with a few exceptions — largely a one-way street.

Morley Callaghan had taken it for granted that a young writer would cut his teeth in the U.S. magazine market, and would go on to be published in New York — the route he himself had taken — but this was an increasingly unlikely scenario.[1] Young Canadian "experimental" writers felt cut off

— too "Canadian," whatever that meant, to be published internationally, and too radical in their approach to their writing to be published readily in the five or so established but beleaguered Canadian English-language houses functioning at that time. These houses estimated — rightly enough — that in such newly postcolonial times, when the "real" cultural places were thought to be elsewhere, the audience for Canadian writing wasn't large enough to justify their investing in a novel unless a foreign publishing partner could be obtained. But, Canada being viewed in "The States" as the place where the snow came from, and "Canadian writer" being considered an oxymoron by London cultural commentators, foreign partners willing to take the chance were few.

If you were a frustrated young writer who despaired of making a place for yourself in Canada, you could always move, of course; you could live elsewhere and begin publishing there, and that's what some novelists did. Or if you were a poet, you could crank out your own work and that of your friends on small presses and stick it into mimeo magazines, such as *Tish* and *The Sheet*, or even into more beautifully-designed productions such as *Emblem Books* and *Alphabet*; there was already a tradition of this sort of publishing in Canada. You could "publish" over the airwaves, on Robert Weaver's show, *Anthology* — about the only venue that would pay you actual money. You could — from 1960 or so on — read your poetry out loud, in a few dark, smoky coffeehouses that held reading series; and there you might meet international — usually American — poets who were blowing through town.

Or you could, alone or together with other writers, scrape together a few dollars and start a new small publishing house. And this is what indeed happened, in more or less that order. Contact Press, Coach House Press, House of Anansi Press, Talonbooks, BlewOintment Press, Sono Nis, and Quarry Press were among the many such enterprises that began in this way at that time. Many but not all of the writers sampled here were also poets, and many of the presses that first published them began with poetry, in the early to mid-60s. The overlaps — poets publishing poets in presses devoted to poetry — were considerable. Michael Ondaatje was for years a member of the Coach House collective; I myself worked as an editor with House of Anansi Press. Andreas Schroeder worked with Sono Nis, George Bowering was associated with *Tish*; and these are just a few examples.

This scene was not idyllic. In my own experience, small-press publishing was a hotbed of jealousy and intrigue and puddles of blood on the floor, second only to Rome under Caligula. Coach House Press got around this in the early days by consuming large amounts of mellowing substances — "Printed in Canada by mindless acid freaks," read their logo, right alongside "Copyright is obsolete" — but at House of Anansi it was not so much drugs as drinking, and no one got out of it without a knife between the shoulder blades. No one but a lunatic, or someone brainwashed by the Girl Guides into thinking she had to do Good Deeds For Others, would have stayed in this situation for long. Which was I? A little of both. But that's another story.

The writers in *Ground Works*, as a group, were born in the 30s or the 40s. They were not baby boomers: they preceded that wave. As children they were close to Depression times, and also to war times, when Canada had in fact cut a bit of a dash. They came of intellectual age at the zenith of the post-war French intellectuals; they read the great modernists as a matter of course. Existentialism was the philosophical catchword then; Brecht and Sartre and the Theatre of the Absurd were frequently performed on campuses, "experiment" was in the air. This period followed the McCarthy years, transited the Age of the Beatniks, and led into days of the Civil Rights movement and then into the era of the Vietnam War. It was a time of ferment and change, and out of that cauldron came — at about this time — the idea of cultural nationalism. This was a modest enough thing in Canada, consisting as it did mainly in a proclamation of one's own existence, but it caused a good deal of uproar nonetheless. (Canada was then, and still is, one of those odd places where large doses of patriotism are considered unpatriotic, and where the powers that be are of the firm belief that a rocked boat always sinks.)

This was also, in writing, perhaps the most thoroughly male-dominated period of the past hundred years. Internationally, the great female modernists belonged to the first third of the twentieth century. (Of the Canadians,

Elizabeth Smart was then unknown, Mavis Gallant, if noticed at all, was believed to be an American, and Sheila Watson had composed *The Double Hook* some time before its ultimate publication in 1961, when it appeared just in time to perk a lot of us up.) The hot new writers making their débuts in the late 40s and the 50s and the early 60s were almost all men. Many reasons could be given for this state of affairs, but suffice it to say that such was the reality, and it — as well as the observable fact that men have historically been more interested in literature as a game than women have been — accounts for the scarcity of female writers in this collection. More women writers of all kinds would appear in Canada shortly. Margaret Laurence would come to prominence, Alice Munro and Marian Engel would publish at the tail end of the 60s, and many more would follow, some of whom wrote "experimental" fiction and are included in this book. But writing in the 60s was pretty much a guy thing, in Canada as elsewhere, in experimental literature as well as in the "mainstream."

It was also an urban thing. The small town, the wilderness, the Native motifs, and the pioneering past of earlier Canadian writing had been tossed out along with the Empire. They'd be back, but they hadn't come back yet.

I've made the literary climate back then sound like inclement weather, and it was. There wasn't much infrastructure or public recognition — writers, when thought about at all, were pictured as bearded maniacs inhabiting some insalubrious bohemia or drafty ivory tower; or, if female, especially if female poets, as half-baked women, the baked half being the head in the oven, for after the recent, spectacular exit of Sylvia Plath, suicide for such was almost de rigeur. Unless you cracked New York — a snowball's chance in hell — there were scant prospects of being rich and famous. But on the other hand it was an era of tremendous freedom. You didn't have to worry about market forces, because there was hardly any market as such: the numbers for even a Canadian "best-seller" were tiny by today's standards. You could travel strange roads, because there were no highways. You didn't feel weighted down by your country's cultural baggage, because — officially at any rate — there wasn't much of it. You could get lost in the language, because the signposts were few. You could take your influences from wherever you liked, because who was looking?

It was a verbal free-for-all: a rambunctious eclecticism prevailed. There was — strangely enough — a spirit of enormous optimism: not much was actual, therefore everything was potential. All was poised on the verge, about to happen. We felt, for a while, as if we really could stop being who we were often told we were — small, boring, hopelessly provincial — and, like the albatross, go straight from fledgling status to full soaring flight.

Ground Works allows us to look back on those simmering years.

(After that, of course, everything changed. As is its habit.)

— MARGARET ATWOOD, 2002

LEONARD COHEN 1934–

Leonard Cohen (b. Montreal, QC) is a celebrated songwriter, who has published many books of poetry, including *Let Us Compare Mythologies* (1956), *The Spice Box of Earth* (1961), *Flowers for Hitler* (1964), *The Energy of Slaves* (1972), *Death of a Lady's Man* (1978), and *Book of Mercy* (1984). His novels include *The Favourite Game* (1963) and *Beautiful Losers* (1966). He declined the Governor General's Award, despite winning it for his *Selected Poems* (1968); however, he accepted the award in 1993 for his career as a vocalist. He has gained global renown for his music, recorded on such albums as *The Songs of Leonard Cohen* (1968), *New Skin for the Old Ceremony* (1974), *Various Positions* (1985), *I'm Your Man* (1988), *The Future* (1992), and *Ten New Songs* (2001).

    Beautiful Losers recounts a cultural allegory about an English Canadian, a French Canadian, and a Native Canadian, all of whom indulge in orgiastic escapades that stem from a universal obsession with the Iroquois saint, Catherine Tekakwitha. Linda Hutcheon has described this delirious, rhapsodic novel as an early Canadian forebear of metafictional postmodernism: "*Beautiful Losers* is a . . . fiction that is also about fiction, that contains within itself a . . . critical commentary on its own nature as narrative."[2] Book Three describes the ultimate exploits of the eremitic narrator, whose unwanted presence at a carnival causes a riot that ends in his own apotheosis at the moment when he suddenly vanishes, transforming himself into a movie that stars Ray Charles.

FROM *BEAUTIFUL LOSERS*
BY LEONARD COHEN

SPRING comes into Québec from the west. It is the warm Japan Current that brings the change of season to the west coast of Canada, and then the West Wind picks it up. It comes across the prairies in the breath of the Chinook, waking up the grain and caves of bears. It flows over Ontario like a dream of legislation, and it sneaks into Québec, into our villages, between our birch trees. In Montréal the cafés, like a bed of tulip bulbs, sprouts from their cellars in a display of awnings and chairs. In Montréal spring is like an autopsy. Everyone wants to see the inside of the frozen mammoth. Girls rip off their sleeves and the flesh is sweet and white, like wood under green bark. From the streets a sexual manifesto rises like an inflating tire, "The winter has not killed us again!" Spring comes into Québec from Japan, and like a pre-war Crackerjack prize it breaks the first day because we play too hard with it. Spring comes into Montréal like an American movie of Riviera Romance, and everyone has to sleep with a foreigner, and suddenly the house lights flare and it's summer, but we don't mind because spring is really a little flashy for our taste, a little effeminate, like the furs of Hollywood lavatories. Spring is an exotic import, like rubber love equipment from Hong Kong, we only want it for a special afternoon, and vote tariffs tomorrow if necessary. Spring passes through our midst like a Swedish tourist co-ed visiting an Italian restaurant for mustache experience, and they assail her with ancient Valentino, of which she chooses one random cartoon. Spring comes to Montréal so briefly you can name the day and plan nothing for it.

It was such a day in a national forest just south of the city. An old man stood in the threshold of his curious abode, a treehouse battered and precarious as a secret boys' club. He did not know how long he had lived there, and he wondered why he no longer fouled the shack with excrement, but he didn't wonder very hard. He sniffed the fragrant western breeze, and he inspected a few pine needles, blackened at their points as if winter had been a brush fire. The young perfume in the air produced no nostalgic hefts in the heart beneath his filthy matted beard. The vaguest mist of pain like lemon squeezed from a distant table caused him to squint his eyes: he scraped his memory for an incident out of his past with which to mythologize the change of season, some honeymoon, or walk, or triumph, that he could let the spring renew, and his pain was finding none. His memory represented no incident, it was all one incident, and it flowed too fast, like the contents of a spittoon in recess jokes. And it seemed only a moment ago that the twenty-below wind had swept through the snow-laden branches of the second-growth fir trees, wind of a thousand whisk brooms raising tiny white hurricanes between the dark of the branches. Beneath him there were still islands of melting snow, like the bellies of beached and corrupted bloated fish. It was a beautiful day as usual.

— Soon it will get warm, he said out loud. Soon I'll begin to stink again, and my thick trousers which are now merely stiff will become sticky, probably. I don't mind.

The obvious problems of the winter he hadn't minded either. It hadn't always been that way, of course. Years (?) back, when some fruitless search or escape had chased him up the trunk, he had hated the cold. The cold seized his shack like a bus stop, and froze him with a fury that was positively personal and petty. The cold chose him like a bullet inscribed with a paraplegic's name. Night after night he cried out in pain during the freezing appliance. But this last winter the cold had only passed through him in its general travels, and he was merely freezing to death. Dream after dream had torn shrieks from his saliva, imploring the name of someone who might have saved him. Morning after morning he rose from soiled leaves and papers which comprised his mattress, frozen snot and tears in his eyebrows. Long ago, the animals fled each time he broke the air with his suffering, but that was when he screamed *for* something. Now that he merely screamed, the rabbits and weasels did not frighten. He presumed that they now accepted his scream as his ordinary bark. And whenever this fine mist of pain made him squint, as it did on this spring day, he stretched open his mouth, torturing the knots of hair on his face, and established his scream throughout the national forest.

— Aaaaaaarrrrrrrggggggghhhhhhhh! Oh, hello!

The scream switched into a salutation as the old man recognized a boy of seven running toward his tree, taking great care to wade through every drift. The child was out of breath as he waved. He was the youngest son of the keeper of a nearby tourist hotel.

— Hi! Hi! Uncle!

The child was not a relative of the old man. He used the word in a charming combination of respect for the anciently and a rubbing of the forefingers in Naughty, Naughty, for he knew the fellow was shameless, and half out of his head.

— Hello, darling boy!

— Hello, Uncle. How is the concussion?

— Climb up! I've missed you. We can get undressed today.

— I can't today, Uncle.

— Please.

— I haven't got time today. Tell me a story, Uncle.

— If you haven't got time to climb up you haven't got time to listen to a story. It's warm enough to get undressed.

— Aw, tell me one of those Indian stories that you often swear you're going to turn into a book one day, as if I cared whether or not you were successful.

— Don't pity me, boy.

— Shut up, you filthy creep!

— Climb up, oh, c'mon. It's a short tree. I'll tell you a story.

— Tell it from up there, if you don't mind, if it's all the same to your itchy fingers, if it's half a dozen and six, I'll squat right where I am.

— Squat here! I'll clear a space.

— Don't make me sick, Uncle. Now let's hear it.

— Be careful! Look at the way you're squatting! You're ruining your little body like that. Keep the thigh muscles engaged. Get the small buttocks away from the heels, keep a healthy space or your buttock muscles will overdevelop.

— They asked me if you ever talk dirty when the children come across you in the woods.

— Who asked you?

— Nobody. Mind if I pee?

— I knew you were a good boy. Watch your leggings. Write your name.

— Story, Uncle! And maybe later I'll say maybe.

— All right. Listen carefully. This is an exciting story:

IROQUOIS	ENGLISH	FRENCH
Ganeagaono	Mohawk	Agnier
Onayotekaono	Oneida	Onneyut
Onundagaono	Onondaga	Onnontagué
Gweugwehono	Cayuga	Goyogouin
Nundawaono	Seneca	Tsonnontouan

The Iroquois ending *ono* (*onon* in French) merely means people.

— Thank you, Uncle. Good-by.

— Do I have to get down on my knees?

— I told you not to say bad words. This morning, I don't know why, but I informed the Provincial Police about us.

— Did you tell them details?

— I had to.

— Such as?

— Such as your cold freakish hand on my little wrinkled scrotum.

— What did they say?

— They said they've suspected you for years.

The old man stood by the highway, jerking his arm in the hitchhiker's signal. Car after car passed him. Drivers that didn't think he was a scarecrow thought he was an outrageously hideous old man, and wouldn't have touched him with *your* door. In the woods behind, a Catholic posse was beating the bushes. The best he could expect at their hands was a death whipping, and to be fondled unspeakably, as the Turks Lawrence. Above him on the electric wires perched the first crows of the year, arranged between the poles like abacus beads. His shoes sucked the water out of the mud like a pair of roots. There would be a mist of pain when he forgot *this* spring, as he must. The traffic was not heavy but it scorned him regularly with little explosions of air as the fenders snapped by. Suddenly, as the action freezing into a still on the movie screen, an Oldsmobile materialized out of the blur streaming past him. There was a beautiful girl behind the wheel, maybe a blonde housewife. Her small hands, which hung lightly from the top of the wheel, were covered with elegant white gloves, and they drifted into her wrists like a pair of perfect bored acrobats. She drove the car effortlessly, like the pointer on a Ouija Board. She wore her hair loose, and she was used to fast cars.

— Climb in, she spoke only to the windshield. Try not to dirty things.

He shoveled himself into the leather seat beside her, having to shut the door several times in order to free his rags. Except for footwear, she was naked below the armrest, and she kept the map light on to be sure you noticed it. As the car pulled away it was pelted with stones and buckshot because the posse had reached the edge of the forest. At top speed he noticed that she had slanted the air ventilator to play on her pubic hair.

— Are you married? he asked.

— What if I am?

— I don't know why I asked. I'm sorry. May I rest my head in your lap?

— They always ask me if I'm married. Marriage is only a symbol for a ceremony which can be exhausted as easily as it can be renewed.

— Spare me your philosophy, Miss.

— You filthy heap! Eat me!

— Gladly.

— Keep your ass off the accelerator.

— Is this right?

— Yah, yah, yah, yah.

— Come forward a little. The leather hurts my chin.

— Have you any idea who I am?

— Ubleubleubleuble — none — ubleubleubleuble.

— Guess! Guess! You thatch of shit!

— I'm not in the least interested.

— Ισις ἐγω —

— Foreigners bore me, Miss.

— Are you quite finished, you foul stump of rot? Yi! Yi! You do it wonderful!

— You ought to use one of those anti-sweat wood ladder seats. Then you wouldn't be sitting in your juices in a draft all day.

— I'm very proud of you, darling. Now get out! Clean up!

— Are we downtown, already?

— We are. Good-by, darling.

— Good-by. Have a magnificent crash.

The old man climbed out of the slow-moving car just in front of the System Theatre. She rammed her moccasin down on the gas pedal and roared into the broadside of a traffic jam in Phillips Square. The old man paused for a moment under the marquee, eyeing the huddled vegetarians with two slight traces, one of nostalgia, one of pity. He forgot them as soon as he bought his ticket. He sat down in the darkness.

— When does the show start, pardon me, sir?

— Are you crazy? And get away from me, you smell terrible.

He changed his seat three or four times waiting for the newsreel to begin. Finally he had the whole front row to himself.

— Usher! Usher!

— Shhh. Quiet!

— Usher! I'm not going to sit here all night. When does the show start?

— You're disturbing the people, sir.

The old man wheeled around and he saw row after row of silent raised eyes, and the occasional mouth chewing mechanically, and the eyes shifted continuously, as if they were watching a small pingpong game. Sometimes, when all the eyes contained exactly the same image, like all the windows of a huge slot machine repeating bells, they made a noise in unison. It only happened when they all saw exactly the same thing, and the noise was called laughter, he remembered.

— The last feature is on, sir.

Now he understood as much as he needed. The movie was invisible to him. His eyes were blinking at the same rate as the shutter in the projector, times per second, and therefore the screen was merely black. It was automatic. Among the audience, one or two viewers, noting their unaccustomed renewal of pleasure during Richard Widmark's maniac laugh in *Kiss of Death*, realized that they were probably in the presence of a Master of the Yoga of the Movie Position. No doubt these students applied themselves to their disciplines with replenished enthusiasm, striving to guarantee the intensity of the flashing story, never imagining that their exercises led, not to perpetual suspense, but to a black screen. For the first time in his life the old man relaxed totally.

— No, sir. You can't change your seat again. Oops, where's he gone? That's funny. Hmmm.

The old man smiled as the flashlight beam went through him.

The hot dogs looked naked in the steam bath of the Main Shooting and Game Alley, an amusement arcade on St. Lawrence Boulevard. The Main Shooting and Game Alley wasn't brand new, and it would never be modernized because only offices could satisfy the rising real estate. The Photomat was broken; it accepted quarters but returned neither flashes nor pictures. The Claw Machine had never obeyed an engineer, and a greasy dust covered the encased old chocolate bars and Japanese Ronsons. There were a few yellow pinball machines of ancient variety, models from before the introduction of flippers. Flippers, of course, have destroyed the sport by legalizing the notion of the second chance. They have weakened the now-or-never nerve of the player and modified the sickening plunge of an unobstructed steel ball. Flippers represent the first totalitarian assault against Crime; by incorporating it into the game mechanically they subvert its old thrill and challenge. Since flippers, no new generation has really mastered the illegal body exertions, and TILT, once as honorable as a saber scar, is no more important than a foul ball. The second chance is the essential criminal idea; it is the lever of heroism, and the only sanctuary of the desperate. But unless it is wrenched from fate, the second chance loses its vitality, and it creates not criminals but nuisances, amateur pickpockets rather than Prometheans. Homage to the Main Shooting and Game Alley, where a man can still be trained. But it was never crowded any more. A few teen-age male prostitutes hung around the warm Peanuts and Assorted machine, boys at the very bottom of Montréal's desire apparatus, and their pimps wore false fur collars and gold teeth and pencil mustaches, and they all stared at the Main (as St. Lawrence Boulevard is called) rather pathetically, as if the tough passing crowds would never disclose the Mississippi Pleasure Boat they might rightfully corrupt. The lighting was early fluorescent, and it did something bad to peroxide hair, it seemed to x-ray the dark roots through the yellow pompadours, and it located every adolescent pimple like a road map. The hot-dog counter, composed mainly of bells and pits of aluminum, exhibited the gray hygiene of slum clinics, which depends on a continual distribution, rather than elimination, of grease. The counter men were tattooed Poles, who hated each other for ancient reasons, and never got in each other's way. They wore the possible uniforms of an infantry of barbers, spoke only Polish and a limited Esperanto of hot-dog conditions. It was no use to complain to one of them over an unanswered dime. An apathetic anarchy mounted OUT OF ORDER signs over the slots of broken telephones and jammed electric shooting galleries. The Bowl-a-Matic habitually divided every strike between First and Second Player regardless of who or how many threw. Still, here and there among the machines of the Main Shooting and Game Alley a true sportsman would be losing coin in gestures that attempted to incorporate decay into game risk, and, when an accurately blasted target did not fold away or light up, he understood it merely as the extension of the game's complexity. Only the hot dogs had not declined, and only because they have no working parts.

— Where do you think you're going, Mister?

— Aw, let him in. It's the first night of spring.

— Listen, we got *some* standards.

— C'mon in, Mister. Have a hot dog on the house.

— No thank you. I don't eat.

As the Poles argued, the old man slipped into the Main Shooting and Game Alley. The pimps let him go by without an obscenity.

— Don't get near him. The guy stinks!

— Get him out of here.

The pile of rags and hair stood before William's De Luxe Polar Hunt. Above the little arctic stage set an unilluminated glass picture represented realistic polar bears, seals, icebergs, and two bearded, quilted American explorers. The flag of their nationality is planted in a drift. In two places the picture gave way to interior-looking windows which registered SCORE and TIME. The mounted pistol pointed at several ranks of movable tin figures. Carefully the old man read the instructions which had been Scotchtaped along with fingerprints to a corner of the glass.

Penguins score 1 point–10 points second time up

Seals score 2 points

Igloo Bull's Eye when entrance is lit, scores 100 points

North Pole when visible, scores 100 points

Walrus appears after North Pole has been hit 5 times & scores 1000 points

Slowly, he committed the instructions to memory, where they merely became part of his game.

— That one's broken, Mister.

The old man pressed his palm against the pineapple grip and hooked his finger on the worn silver trigger.

— Look at his hand!

— It's all burnt!

— He's got no thumb!

— Isn't he the Terrorist Leader that escaped tonight?

— Looks more like the pervert they showed on TV they're combing the country for.

— Get him out!

— He stays! He's a Patriot!

— He's a stinking cocksucker!

— He's very nearly the President of our country!

Just as the staff and clientele of the Main Shooting and Game Alley were to succumb to a sordid political riot, something very remarkable happened to the old man. Twenty men were swarming toward him, half to expel the disgusting intruder, half to restrain the expulsionists and consequently to boost the noble heap on their shoulders. In a split second the traffic had stopped on the Main, and a crowd was threatening the steamy plate windows. For the first time in their lives, twenty men experienced the delicious certainty that they were at the very center of action, no matter which side. A cry of happiness escaped from each man as he closed in on his object. Already an accumulation of tangled sirens had provoked the strolling mob like an orchestra at a bull fight. It was the first night of spring, the streets belong to the People! Blocks away, a policeman pocketed his badge and opened his collar. Hard women in ticket booths sized up the situation, whispering to the ushers as they secured their plow-shaped wood window plugs. The theaters began to empty because they face the wrong way. Action was suddenly in the streets! They could all sense it as they closed in on the Main: something was happening in Montréal history! A bitter smile could be detected on the lips of trained revolutionaries and Witnesses of Jehovah, who immediately dispatched all their pamphlets in one confetti salutation. Every man who was a terrorist in his heart whispered, At Last. The police assembled toward the commotion, ripping insignia away like it was scabs which could be traded, but preserving their platoon formations, in order to offer an unidentified discipline to serve whatever ruled next. Poets arrived hoping to turn the expected riot into a rehearsal. Mothers came forth to observe whether they had toilet-trained their sons for the right crisis. Doctors appeared in great numbers, natural enemies of order. The business community attained the area in a disguise of consumers. Androgynous hashish smokers rushed in for a second chance at fuck. All the second chancers rushed in, the divorced, the converted, the overeducated, they all rushed in for their second chance, karate masters, adult stamp collectors, Humanists, give us, give us our second chance! It was the Revolution! It was the first night of spring, the night of small religions. In another month there would be fireflies and lilacs. An entire cult of Tantric love perfectionists turned exocentric in their second chance at compassion, destroying public structures of selfish love with beautiful displays of an acceptable embrace for street intercourse of genitalia. A small Nazi Party of adolescents felt like statesmen as they defected to the living mob. The Army hovered over the radio, determining if the situation was intensely historical, in which case it would overtake Revolution with the Tortoise of a Civil War. Professional actors, all performing artists including magicians, rushed in for their last and second chance.

— Look at him!

— What's happening?

Between the De Luxe Polar Hunt and the plate-glass windows of the Main Shooting and Game Alley the gasps were beginning that would spread over the heads of the astounded crowd like a leak in the atmosphere. The old man had commenced his remarkable performance (which I do not intend to describe). Suffice it to say that he disintegrated slowly; just as a crater extends its circumference with endless tiny landslides along the rim, he dissolved from the inside out. His presence had not completely disappeared when he began to reassemble himself. "Had not completely disappeared" is actually the wrong way of looking at it. His presence was like the shape of an hourglass, strongest where it was smallest. And that point where he was most absent, that's when the gasps started, because the future streams through that point, going both ways. That is the beautiful waist of the hourglass! That is the point of Clear Light! Let it change forever what we do not know! For a lovely briefness all the sand is compressed in the stem between the two flasks! Ah, this is not a second chance. For all the time it takes to launch a sigh he allowed the spectators a vision of All Chances At Once! For some purists (who merely destroy shared information by mentioning it) this point of most absence was the feature of the evening. Quickly now, as if even he participated in the excitement over the unknown, he greedily reassembled himself into — into a movie of Ray Charles. Then he enlarged the screen, degree by degree, like a documentary on the Industry. The moon occupied one lens of his sunglasses, and he laid out his piano keys across a shelf of the sky, and he leaned over him as though they were truly the row of giant fishes to feed a hungry multitude. A fleet of jet planes dragged his voice over us who were holding hands.

— Just sit back and enjoy it, I guess.

— Thank God it's only a movie.

— Hey! cried a New Jew, laboring on the lever of the broken Strength Test. Hey. Somebody's making it!

The end of this book has been rented to the Jesuits. The Jesuits demand the official beatification of Catherine Tekakwitha!

"Pour le succes de l'enterprise, for the success of this enterprise, il est essential que les miracles éclatent de nouveau, it is essential that the miracles sparkle again, et donc que le culte de la sainte grandisse, and thus extend the cult of the saint, qu'on l'invoque partout avec confiance, that one may invoke her with confidence everywhere, qu'elle redevienne par son invocation, that she becomes again by her mere invocation, par les reliques, by her relics, par la poudre de son tombeau, by the dust of her grave, la semeuse de miracles qu'elle fut au temps jadis, the sower of miracles that she was in former times." We petition the country for miracle evidence, *and we submit this document, whatever its intentions, as the first item in a revived testimonial to the Indian girl.*

"Le Canada et Les États-Unis puiseront de nouvelles forces au contact de ce lis très pur des bords de la Mohawk et des rives du Saint-Laurent. Canada and the United States will achieve a new strength from contact with this purest lily from the shores of the Mohawk and the banks of the St. Lawrence River."

Poor men, poor men, such as we, they've gone and fled. I will plead from electrical tower. I will plead from turret of plane. He will uncover His face. He will not leave me alone. I will spread His name in Parliament. I will welcome His silence in pain. I have come through the fire of family and love. I smoke with my darling, I sleep with my friend. We talk of the poor men, broken and fled. Alone with my radio I lift up my hands. Welcome to you who read me today. Welcome to you who put my heart down. Welcome to you, darling and friend, who miss me forever in your trip to the end.

AUDREY THOMAS 1935–

Audrey Thomas (b. Binghamton, NY) has published numerous books, including *Ten Green Bottles* (1967), *Mrs. Blood* (1970), *Songs My Mother Taught Me* (1973), *Blown Figures* (1974), *Ladies and Escorts* (1977), *Latakia* (1979), *Real Mothers* (1981), *Goodbye Harold, Good Luck* (1986), *Graven Images* (1993), *Isobel Gunn* (1999), and *The Path of Totality* (2001). She has won the Ethel Wilson Award three times for her works of fiction: once for *Intertidal Life* (1985), once for *Wild Blue Yonder* (1991), and once for *Coming Down from Wa* (1995). She is also the recipient of the Marian Engel Award (1987), the Canada-Australia Prize (1989), and the W. O. Mitchell Award (2001). She is an itinerant instructor of creative writing.

"If One Green Bottle . . ." itemizes a broken series of lyrical phrases, all of which evoke the mental trauma of a woman giving birth to a stillborn child. Thomas has equated the act of writing to a kind of vivisection, and she remarks: "I quite literally cut things up and paste them into place."[3] Her narrative thus takes the form of a stream-of-consciousness, in which the protagonist expresses both agony and grief through a hybrid tissue of fragmented references, all quoted from biblical tales, hellenic myths, and childish songs. The repeated ellipsis almost becomes a kind of marker for the pulses of breath taken between each exclamation and contraction. The story in effect constitutes an allegory about the poetic labour of the writer, who responds to a mortal loss by creating a living work.

"IF ONE GREEN BOTTLE . . ."
FROM *TEN GREEN BOTTLES*
BY AUDREY THOMAS

WHEN fleeing, one should never look behind. Orpheus, Lot's wife . . . penalties grotesque and terrible await us all. It does not pay to doubt . . . to turn one's head . . . to rely on the confusion . . . the smoke . . . the fleeing multitudes . . . the satisfaction of the tumbling cities . . . to distract the attention of the gods. Argus-eyed, they wait, he waits . . . the golden chessmen spread upon the table . . . the opponent's move already known, accounted for. . . . Your pawns, so vulnerable . . . advancing with such care (if you step on a crack, then you'll break your mother's back). Already the monstrous hand trembles in anticipation . . . the thick lips twitch with suppressed laughter . . . then pawn, knight, castle, queen scooped up and tossed aside. "Check," and (click click) "check . . . mmmate." The game is over, and you . . . surprised (but why?) . . . petulant . . . your nose still raw from the cold . . . your galoshes not yet dried . . . really, it's indecent . . . inhumane (why bother to come? answer: the bother of not coming) . . . and not even the offer of a sandwich or a cup of tea . . . discouraging . . . disgusting. The great mouth opens . . . like a whale really . . . he strains you, one more bit of plankton, through his teeth (my mother had an ivory comb once). "Next week . . . ? At the same time . . . ? No, no, not at all. I do not find it boring in the least. . . . Each time a great improvement. Why, soon," the huge lips tremble violently, "ha, ha, you'll be beating me." Lies . . . all lies. Yet, even as you go, echoes of Olympian laughter in your ears, you know you will return, will once more challenge . . . and be defeated once again. Even plankton have to make a protest . . . a

19

stand . . . what else can one do? "Besides, it passes the time . . . keeps my hand in . . . and you never know. . . . One time, perhaps . . . a slip . . . a flutter of the eyelids. . . . Even the gods grow old."

The tropical fan, three-bladed, omniscient, omnipotent, inexorable, churns up dust and mosquitoes, the damp smell of coming rain, the overripe smell of vegetation, of charcoal fires, of human excrement, of fear . . . blown in through the open window, blown up from the walls and the floor. All is caught in the fan's embrace, the efficient arms of the unmoved mover. The deus in the machina, my old chum the chess-player, refuses to descend . . . yet watches. Soon they will let down the nets and we will lie in the darkness, in our gauze houses, like so many lumps of cheese . . . protected . . . revealed. The night-fliers, dirty urchins, will press their noses at my windows and lick their hairy lips in hunger . . . in frustration. Can they differentiate, I wonder, between the blood of my neighbor and mine? Are there aesthetes among the insects who will touch only the soft parts . . . between the thighs . . . under the armpits . . . along the inner arm? Are there vintages and connoisseurs? I don't like the nights here: that is why I wanted it over before the night. One of the reasons. If I am asleep I do not know who feeds on me, who has found the infinitesimal rip and invited his neighbors in. Besides, he promised it would be over before the night. And one listens, doesn't one? . . . one always believes. . . . Absurd to rely on verbal consolation . . . clichés so worn they feel like old coins . . . smooth . . . slightly oily to the touch . . . faceless.

Pain, the word, I mean, derived (not according to Skeat) from "pay" and "Cain." How can there, then, be an exit . . . a way out? The darker the night, the clearer the mark on the forehead . . . the brighter the blind man's cane at the crossing . . . the louder the sound of footsteps somewhere behind. Darkness heightens the absurd sense of "situation" . . . gives the audience its kicks. But tonight . . . really . . . All Souls' . . . it's too ridiculous. . . . Somebody goofed. The author has gone too far; the absurdity lies in one banana skin, not two or three. After one, it becomes too painful . . . too involved . . . too much like home. Somebody will have to pay for this . . . the reviews . . . tomorrow . . . all will be most severe. The actors will sulk over their morning cup of coffee . . . the angel will beat his double breast above the empty pocketbook . . . the director will shout and stamp his feet. . . . The whole thing should have been revised . . . rewritten . . . we knew it from the first.

(This is the house that Jack built. This is the cat that killed the rat that lived in the house that Jack built. We are the maidens all shaven and shorn, that milked the cow with the crumpled horn . . . that loved in the hearse that Joke built. Excuse me, please, was this the Joke that killed the giant or the Jack who tumbled down . . . who broke his crown? Crown him with many crowns, the lamb upon his throne. He tumbled too . . . it's inevitable. . . . It all, in the end, comes back to the nursery. . . . Jill, Humpty Dumpty, Rock-a-bye baby . . . they-kiss-you, they-kiss-you . . . they all fall down. The nurses in the corner playing Ludo . . . centurions dicing. We are all betrayed by Cock-a-Doodle-Doo. . . . We all fall down. Why, then, should I be exempt? . . . presumptuous of me . . . please forgive.)

Edges of pain. Watch it, now, the tide is beginning to turn. Like a cautious bather, stick in one toe . . . both feet . . . "brr" . . . the impact of the ocean . . . the solidity of the thing, now that you've finally got under . . . like swimming in an ice cube really. "Yes, I'm coming. Wait for me." The shock of the total immersion . . . the pain breaking over the head. Don't cry out . . . hold your breath . . . so. "Not so bad, really, when one gets used to it." That's it . . . just the right tone . . . the brave swimmer. . . . Now wave a gay hand toward the shore. Don't let them know . . . the indignities . . . the chattering teeth . . . the blue lips . . . the sense of isolation. . . . Good.

And Mary, how did she take it, I wonder, the original, the appalling announcement . . . the burden thrust upon her? "No, really, some other time . . . the spring planting . . . my aged mother . . . quite impossible. Very good of you to think of me, of course, but I couldn't take it on. Perhaps you'd call in again next year." (Dismiss him firmly . . . quickly, while there's still time. Don't let him get both feet in the door. Be firm and final. "No, I'm sorry, I never accept free gifts.") And then the growing awareness, the anger showing quick and hot under the warm brown of the cheeks. The voice . . . like oil. . . . "I'm afraid I didn't make myself clear." (Like the detective novels. . . . "Allow me to present my card . . . my credentials." The shock of recognition . . . the horror. "Oh, I see. . . . Yes . . . well, if it's like that. . . . Come this way." A gesture of resignation. She allows herself one sigh . . . the ghost of a smile.) But no, it's all wrong. Mary . . . peasant girl . . . quite a different reaction implied. Dumbfounded . . . remember Zachary. A shocked silence . . . the rough fingers twisting together like snakes . . . awe . . . a certain rough pride ("Wait until I tell the other girls. The well . . . tomorrow morning. . . . I won't be proud about it, not really. But it is an honor. What will Mother say?") *Droit de seigneur* . . . the servant summoned to the bedchamber . . . honored . . . afraid. Or perhaps like Leda. No preliminaries . . . no thoughts at all. Too stupid . . . too frightened . . . the thing was, after all, over so quickly. That's it . . . stupidity . . . the necessary attribute. I can hear him now. "That girl . . . whatzername? . . . Mary. Mary will do. Must be a simple woman. . . . That's where we made our first mistake. Eve too voluptuous . . . too intelligent . . . this time nothing must go wrong."

And the days were accomplished. Unfair to gloss that over . . . to make so little of the waiting . . . the months . . . the hours. They make no mention of the hours; but of course, men wrote it down. How were they to know? After the immaculate conception, after the long and dreadful journey, after the refusal at the inn . . . came the maculate delivery . . . the manger. And all that noise . . . cattle lowing (and doing other things besides) . . . angels blaring away . . . the eerie light. No peace . . . no chance for sleep . . . for rest between the pains . . . for time to think . . . to gather courage. Yet why should she be afraid . . . downhearted . . . ? Hadn't she had a sign . . . the voice . . . the presence of the star? (And notice well, they never told her about the other thing . . . the third act.) It probably seemed worth it at the time . . . the stench . . . the noise . . . the pain.

Robert the Bruce . . . Constantine . . . Noah. The spider . . . the flaming cross . . . the olive branch. . . . With these signs. . . . I would be content with something far more simple. A breath of wind on the cheek . . . the almost imperceptible movement of a curtain . . . a single flash of lightning.

Courage consists, perhaps, in the ability to recognize signs . . . the symbolism of the spider. But for me . . . tonight . . . what is there? The sound of far-off thunder . . . the smell of coming rain which will wet, but not refresh . . . that tropical fan. The curtain moves . . . yes, I will allow you that. But for me . . . tonight . . . there is only a rat behind the arras. Jack's rat. This time there is no exit . . . no way out or up.

(You are not amused by my abstract speculations? Listen . . . I have more. Time. Time is an awareness, either forward or backward, of Then, as opposed to Now . . . the stasis. Time is the moment between thunder and lightning . . . the interval at the street corner when the light is amber, neither red nor green, but shift gears, look both ways . . . the oasis of pleasure between pains . . . the space between the darkness and the dawn . . . the conversations between courses . . . the fear in the final stroke of twelve . . . the nervous fumbling with cloth and buttons, before the longed-for contact of the flesh . . . the ringing telephone . . . the solitary coffee cup . . . the oasis of pleasure between pains. Time . . . and time again.)

That time when I was eleven and at Scout camp . . . marching in a dusty serpentine to the fire tower . . . the hearty counselors with sun-streaked hair and muscular thighs . . . enjoying themselves, enjoying ourselves . . . the long hike almost over. "Ten green bottles standing on the wall. Ten green bottles standing on the wall. If one green bottle . . . should accidentally fall, there'd be nine green bottles standing on the wall." And that night . . . after pigs in blankets . . . cocoa . . . campfire songs . . . the older girls taught us how to faint . . . to hold our breath and count to thirty . . . then blow upon our thumbs. Gazing up at the stars . . . the sudden sinking back into warmth and darkness . . . the recovery . . . the fresh attempt . . . delicious. In the morning we climbed the fire tower (and I, afraid to look down or up, climbing blindly, relying on my sense of touch), reached the safety of the little room on top. We peered out the windows at the little world below . . . and found six baby mice, all dead . . . curled up, like dust kitties in the kitchen drawer. "How long d'you suppose they've been there?" "Too long. Ugh." "Throw them away." "Put them back where you found them." Disturbed . . . distressed . . . the pleasure marred. "Let's toss them down on Rachel. She was too scared to climb the tower. Baby." "Yes, let's toss them down. She ought to be paid back." (Everything all right now . . . the day saved. Ararat . . . Areopagus. . . .) Giggling, invulnerable, we hurled the small bodies out the window at the Lilliputian form below. Were we punished? Curious . . . I can't remember. And yet the rest . . . so vivid . . . as though it were yesterday . . . this morning . . . five minutes ago. . . . We must have been punished. Surely they wouldn't let us get away with that?

Waves of pain now . . . positive whitecaps . . . breakers. . . . Useless to try to remember . . . to look behind . . . to think. Swim for shore. Ignore the ringing in the ears . . . the eyes half blind with water . . . the waves breaking over the head. Just keep swimming . . . keep moving forward . . . rely on instinct . . . your sense of direction . . . don't look back or forward . . . there isn't time for foolish speculation. . . . See? Flung up . . . at last . . . exhausted, but on the shore. Flotsam . . . jetsam . . . but there, you made it. Lie still.

The expected disaster is always the worst. One waits for it . . . is obsessed by it . . . it nibbles at the consciousness. Jack's rat. Far better the screech of brakes . . . the quick embrace of steel and shattered glass . . . or the sudden stumble from the wall. One is prepared through being unprepared. A few thumps of the old heart . . . like a brief flourish of announcing trumpets . . . a roll of drums . . . and then nothing. This way . . . tonight . . . I wait for the crouching darkness like a child waiting for that movement from the shadows in the corner of the bedroom. It's all wrong . . . unfair . . . there ought to be a law. . . . One can keep up only a given number of chins . . . one keeps silent only a given number of hours. After that, the final humiliation . . . the loss of self-control . . . the oozing out upon the pavement. . . . Dumpty-like, one refuses (or is unable?) to be reintegrated . . . whimpers for morphia and oblivion . . . shouts and tears her hair. . . . That must not happen . . . Undignified . . . déclassé. I shall talk to my friend the fan . . . gossip with the night-fliers . . . pit my small light against the darkness, a miner descending the shaft. I have seen the opening gambit . . . am aware of the game's inevitable conclusion. What does it matter? I shall leap over the net . . . extend my hand . . . murmur, "Well done," and walk away, stiff-backed and shoulders high. I will drink the hemlock gaily . . . I will sing. Ten green bottles standing on the wall. Ten green bottles standing on the wall. If one green bottle should accidentally fall. . . . When it is over I will sit up and call for tea . . . ignore the covered basin . . . the bloody sheets (but what do they do with it afterward . . . where will they take it? I have no experience in these matters). They will learn that the death of a part is not the death of the whole. The tables will be turned . . . and overturned. The shield of Achilles will compensate for his heel.

And yet, were we as innocent as all that . . . as naive . . . that we never wondered where the bottles came from? I never wondered. . . . I accepted them the way a small child draws the Christmas turkey . . . brings the turkey home . . . pins it on the playroom wall . . . and then sits down to eat. One simply doesn't connect. Yet there they were . . . lined up on the laboratory wall . . . half-formed, some of them . . . the tiny vestigial tails of the smallest . . . like corpses of stillborn kittens . . . or baby mice. Did we think that they had been like that always . . . swimming forever in their little formaldehyde baths . . . ships in bottles . . . snowstorms in glass paperweights? The professor's voice . . . droning like a complacent bee . . . tapping his stick against each fragile glass shell . . . cross-pollinating facts with facts . . . our pencils racing over the paper. We accepted it all without question . . . even went up afterward for a closer look . . . boldly . . . without hesitation. It was all so simple . . . so uncomplex . . . so scientific. Stupidity, the necessary attribute. And once we dissected a guinea pig, only to discover that she had been pregnant . . . tiny little guinea pigs inside. We . . . like children presented with one of those Russian dolls . . . were delighted . . . gratified. We had received a bonus . . . a free gift.

Will they do that to part of me? How out of place it will look, bottled with the others . . . standing on the laboratory wall. Will the black professor . . . the brown-eyed students . . . bend their delighted eyes upon this bonus, this free gift? (White. 24 weeks. Female . . . or male.) But perhaps black babies are white . . . or pink . . . to begin. It is an interesting problem . . . one which could be pursued . . . speculated upon. I must ask someone. If black babies are not black before they are born, at what stage does the dark hand of heredity . . . of race . . . touch their small bodies? At the moment of birth perhaps? . . . like silver exposed to the air. But remember their palms . . . the soles of their feet. It's an interesting problem. And remember the beggar outside the central post office . . . the terrible burned place on his arm . . . the new skin . . . translucent . . . almost a shell pink. I turned away in disgust . . . wincing at the shared memory of scalding liquid . . . the pain. But really . . . in retrospect . . . it was beautiful. That pink skin . . . that delicate . . . Turneresque tint . . . apple blossoms against dark branches.

That's it . . . just the right tone. . . . Abstract speculation on birth . . . on death . . . on human suffering in general. Remember only the delicate tint . . . sunset against a dark sky . . . the pleasure of the Guernica. It's so simple, really . . . all a question of organization . . . of aesthetics. One can so easily escape the unpleasantness . . . the shock of recognition. Cleopatra in her robes . . . her crown. . . . "I have immortal longings in me." No fear . . . the asp suckles peacefully and unreproved. . . . She wins . . . and Caesar loses. Better than Falstaff babbling "of green fields." One needs the transcendentalism of the tragic hero. Forget the old man . . . pathetic . . . deserted . . . broken. The gray iniquity. It's all a question of organization . . . of aesthetics . . . of tone. Brooke, for example. "In that rich earth a richer dust concealed. . . ." Terrified out of his wits, of course, but still organizing . . . still posturing.

(The pain is really quite bad now . . . you will excuse me for a moment? I'll be back. I must not think for a moment . . . must not struggle . . . must let myself be carried over the crest of the wave . . . face downward . . . buoyant . . . a badge of seaweed across the shoulder. It's easier this way . . . not to think . . . not to struggle. . . . It's quicker . . . it's more humane.)

Still posturing. See the clown . . . advancing slowly across the platform . . . dragging the heavy rope. . . . Grunts . . . strains . . . the audience shivering with delight. Then the last . . . the desperate . . . tug. And what revealed? . . . a carrot . . . a bunch of grapes . . . a small dog . . . nothing. The audience in tears. . . . "Oh, God . . . how funny. . . . One knows, of course . . . all the time. And yet it never fails to amuse . . . I never fail to be taken in." Smothered giggles in the darkened taxi . . . the deserted streets. . . . "Oh, God, how amusing. . . . Did you see? The carrot . . . the bunch of grapes . . . the small dog . . . nothing. All a masquerade . . . a charade . . . the rouge. . . the powder . . . the false hair of an old woman . . . a clown." Babbling of green fields.

Once, when I was ten, I sat on a damp rock and watched my father fishing. Quiet . . . on a damp rock . . . I watched the flapping gills . . . the frenzied tail . . . the gasps for air . . . the refusal to accept the hook's reality. Rainbow body swinging through the air . . . the silver drops . . . like tears. Watching quietly from the haven of my damp rock, I saw my father struggle with the fish . . . the chased and beaten silver body. "Papa, let it go, Papa . . . please!" My father . . . annoyed . . . astonished . . . his communion disrupted . . . his chalice overturned . . . his paten trampled underfoot. He let it go . . . unhooked it carelessly and tossed it lightly toward the center of the pool. After all, what did it matter . . . to please the child . . . and the damage already done. No recriminations . . . only, perhaps (we never spoke of it), a certain loss of faith . . . a fall, however imperceptible . . . from grace?

The pain is harder now . . . more frequent . . . more intense. Don't think of it . . . ignore it . . . let it come. The symphony rises to its climax. No more andante . . . no more moderato . . . clashing cymbals . . . blaring horns. . . . Lean forward in your seat . . . excited . . . intense . . . a shiver of fear . . . of anticipation. The conductor . . . a wild thing . . . a clockwork toy gone mad. . . . Arms flailing . . . body arched . . . head swinging loosely . . . dum de dum de DUM DUM DUM. The orchestra . . . the audience . . . all bewitched . . . heads nodding . . . fingers moving, yes, oh, yes . . . the orgasm of sound . . . the straining . . . letting go. An ecstasy . . . a crescendo . . . a coda . . . it's over. "Whew." "Terrific." (Wiping the sweat from their eyes.) Smiling . . . self-conscious . . . a bit embarrassed now. . . . "Funny how you can get all worked up over a bit of music." Get back to the formalities. . . . Get off the slippery sand . . . onto the warm, safe planks of conversation. "Would you like a coffee . . . a drink . . . an ice?" The oasis of pleasure between pains. For me, too, it will soon be over . . . and for you.

Noah on Ararat . . . high and dry . . . sends out the dove to see if it is over. Waiting anxiously . . . the dove returning with the sign. Smug now . . . self-satisfied . . . know-it-all. . . . All those drowned neighbors . . . all those doubting Thomases . . . gone . . . washed away . . . full fathoms five. . . . And he, safe . . . the animals pawing restlessly, scenting freedom after their long confinement . . . smelling the rich smell of spring . . . of tender shoots. Victory . . . triumph . . . the chosen ones. Start again . . . make the world safe for democracy . . . cleansing . . . purging . . . Guernica . . . Auschwitz . . . God's fine Italian hand. Always the moral . . . the little tag . . . the cautionary tale. Willie in one of his bright new sashes/fell in the fire and was burnt to ashes. . . . Suffering is good for the soul . . . the effects on the body are not to be considered. Fire and rain . . . cleansing . . . purging . . . tempering the steel. Not much longer now . . . and soon they will let down the nets. (He promised it would be over before the dark. I do not like the dark here. Forgive me if I've mentioned this before.) We will sing to keep our courage up. Ten green bottles standing on the wall. Ten green bottles standing on the wall. If one green bottle. . . .

The retreat from Russia . . . feet bleeding on the white snow . . . tired . . . discouraged . . . what was it all about anyway? . . . we weren't prepared. Yet we go on . . . feet bleeding on the white snow . . . dreaming of warmth . . . smooth arms and golden hair . . . a glass of kvass. We'll get there yet. (But will we ever be the same?) A phoenix . . . never refusing . . . flying true and straight . . . into the fire and out. Plunge downward now . . . a few more minutes . . . spread your wings . . . the moment has come . . . the fire blazes . . . the priest is ready . . . the worshipers are waiting. The battle over . . . the death within expelled . . . cast out . . . the long hike over . . . Ararat. Sleep now . . . and rise again from the dying fire . . . the ashes. It's over . . . eyes heavy . . . body broken but relaxed. All over. We made it, you and I. . . . It's all, is it not . . . a question of organization . . . of tone? Yet one would have been grateful . . . at the last . . . for a reason . . . an explanation . . . a sign. A spider . . . a flaming cross . . . a carrot . . . a bunch of grapes . . . a small dog. Not this nothing.

GRAEME GIBSON 1934–

Graeme Gibson (b. London, ON) has written four novels, which include *Five Legs* (1969), *Communion* (1971), *Perpetual Motion* (1982), and *Gentleman Death* (1993). Gibson has won the Harbourfront Festival Prize (1993), and the Toronto Arts Award (1990). He is also the first recipient of the eponymous Graeme Gibson Award (granted by the Writers' Union of Canada in 1991), and he is a Member of the Order of Canada (1992). He has promoted the political interests of Canadian writers by chairing the Writers' Union of Canada (1974–75), the Book & Periodical Council (1975), and the Writers' Development Trust (1978). He has also served as the president of PEN Canada (1987–89).

    Five Legs is an iconoclastic, experimental narrative about two English academics, Lucan Crackell and Felix Oswald, both of whom suffer from the same kind of dreary tedium that plagues J. Alfred Prufrock. Gibson claims that *Five Legs* models itself upon *Venus and Adonis* by Shakespeare,[4] except that Gibson retells this tale through a stream-of-consciousness, whose modernist overtones evoke the mental milieu of Joyce and Eliot. The excerpt takes place during a road trip to a wintery funeral, when Lucan, the driver, is daydreaming about Vera, an early lover, lost to him because of her refusal to abort an undesired pregnancy; however, this daydream is interrupted when Felix demands that Lucan stop the car so that they might assist another driver, hurt at the side of the road.

FROM *FIVE LEGS*
BY GRAEME GIBSON

CAN'T have, it must be on ahead. Therethere Vera. What, jeez, can I say? Poor lost, my poor lost, my poor lost love on your brutal day. There Vera. There. Clumsy futile, what can I. Soon be. It will be all over soon. Before you know it. Filled with love and sickness, fear around my heart. The town, they know, they must. Lace-curtained watchers under shingled roofs, at strangers' cars that stop before this winterpeeled and battered door with broken gingerbread above, along the eaves. My foot at an ornate scraper for the mud that clings and glancing, a glance at Vera huddled in the car. Pale too, my face I'm sure and glistening whitely. Jeez, I feel so. Waving my hand back but she doesn't see, or perhaps. Perhaps she doesn't want to anymore and Lucan cautiously, dear God my heart transported by these muddy feet! Cautiously into this cluttered unprofessional room, with. Good Lord! Antimacassars for chrissakes and tiptoeing, I'm tiptoeing over to this little bell. Ring and be seated. Eat me. So silent with the feet of mice in the walls. Careful finger, quietly, careful finger unwilling on the. RRRINGGG! Aargh! Good grief it's right. Wow! What a. Right above my frigging head. Lucan sitting dutifully, uncertain on this patch-worked afghan and, tensing, leaping to his feet with cushions scattered to the floor as bursting through the door he comes. Good morning, ha! Good morning, my boy. Bending, Lucan bending to retrieve the yellow satin, purple and yellow cushion by his feet. Don't worry, don't worry about that and clutching my hand, shaking intimately. You phoned me last night? Anguished with the cushion in my arm; pale face and moist pale hand, he.

Yes. Yes, you see we. Garish and lumpy. Blurred reproduction, three colours, of Niagara Falls. You see, we need. Oh God!

I know and when people are in trouble. Glittering eyes, tiny, and rimless glasses; pudgy hand on his heart, a moment. They come to me. From all over they come to me. And do you know why? Do you know why they come from as far away as Detroit? Two and three times, some of them, do you know why, eh? Eyes wet staring into mine; tiny eyes that wait.

No I, I can't say that I.

Because I do a good job, that's why! You notice, confidential lowering of his voice and jerking to the window, peering out, you notice that I haven't asked your name. Bent and turning from the curtain's lace he slowly winks, a long grotesque staring wink. Anonymity. He winks again with screwed up mouth and puffy cheeks. That's right, I try to use a little modern psychology to ease the burdens my patients bear. Oh I know, alright, how people feel when they come to me. I certainly do. Stepping forward in the room, I know how you feel! Yes I do, I do indeed, how much you need me now and I respect. Eager in the dark, mice beneath the floorboards scamper; lace-filtered parlour light, the shadows cornered in this room and pale, she's huddled, twisting there. Clearly. Tried, I've really, and it was yours. Eyes that standing stare, wet watching eyes and Lucan wilting, surrounded by accusations; terror and the rodent feet. Say, where you kids from?

Toronto.

Don't. Raised hands protectively, he turns to stare. Don't tell me about Toronto! Go down, I have to go down at least once a week. Sister-in-law's there, my oldest brother's widow, you know, and she. Gracious! I'm telling you, well. Intimate hand beside his voice, he leans. She doesn't drink to drown her sorrows; she drinks to forget. It's disgusting. Headshaking now, reproval and the twittering feet. And I have to drive down with her, with her supply I guess you'd call it. Ha-ha. Twice a week sometimes. She belts it back for a, why she must be, aah. Seventy-seven, yes. Seventy-seven if she's a day, my brother was. How can he, what's he? Swallowing, Lucan Crackell's focused on the civic pledge that framed and hanging, oozes laurel vined and smiling on the wall. Perhaps it's, you might think it's unkind of me to talk this way about family. But I'm fed up, fed right up here. Do you know, indignant voice, she doesn't even put the exchange on her cheques! Pretty cheap, eh? And it's not as if. She's got, why my brother left her very well set up, very well indeed I might say. He was insurance, you know, and a real go-getter, believe me! Shouting yet she doesn't even, I have to pay the exchange! That's what really takes the cake, you'd think after driving my poor brother, she drove him right into his grave, and make no mistake! Abruptly stopping. The shouting settles and his eyes are blank as pennies. Then, agitated in his corpulence, he zig-zags quickly into the room, he stops and staring at the wall. His wavering voice. You'd think she'd at least pay the exchange. Turning hopelessly and Lucan has to look away. It's only fifteen cents, after all. Fifteen lousy cents. That's not too much to expect is it?

I wave and she doesn't come: beckoning but she shakes her head, so muddy-footed once again I walk to the splattered dripping car. Changed your mind, but? But. Not going, I've decided I'm not going in. Good Lord! Overflowing ashes from the dashboard tray and they've fallen where I've thrown them on the floor: her certain, apologetic face; I'm sorry Lucan, I really am but I won't go in. Crossed her plump legs shining in the sun, it's warm on my back. After all this and she. What are we going to do? But Vera, he's. He's not a bad guy and I'm sure, I know he. What on earth are we going to do? Lucan straining suddenly to see, for what's that, its a. Good God! Couldn't be. Wheels still turning and it's on its back, a monstrous insect helpless on its back. Black and cream, its armour crumpled round the head and now their voices trumpet in. Babble in my ears. Skid marks and there's nobody, not a frigging soul! Oh how terrible. Braking automatically we slow. "No, couldn't be, it must be old, there's no one here."

"But the wheels. They're turning." Grim circles and she's right, dear God, she is. The wind! And they've all gone away, sure. That's it, they've left already. Frig the wheels and boy what a relief that was!

"There's somebody in the back seat." Trust him for chrissakes, trust him! A figure? Nonononono, couldn't be, they've all. Accelerating, bastard

Oswald, past the crippled hulk, brute black and turning in the snow, accelerating for we must get on; they'll all be waiting! Sickness, I'm; nausea burns the throat and my threatening bowels. Couldn't be dear God, bunch of blankets, yes cartons. Or something. My stomach! Sure that's what it is. "Aren't you going to stop?" Now don't my boy, don't get shrill with, what a! Couldn't possibly be. "I said aren't you." Rising accusation, insubordination that I won't forget if you keep it up. Chewing inside, but there would have been someone, someone else, there. Accusatory, don't you raise your; now his hands are pulling at the seat! "You can't just, just drive away for chrissakes, there was someone. There was somebody in the back seat." Police. Police and ambulance, we'll inform them and we're almost there. "I saw, Doctor Crackell I saw, just as clearly as, as anything, a body! I'm sure there's somebody . . ."

"Now, now. Just a minute Oswald, don't, don't fly off the handle. Two things, there are two things. No three things." No three things. Receding in the mirror, dark in the gusts and there's a, he'll stop and see! There's another. Car. "Firstly. And I may be wrong here. I think you're mistaken, I don't." He'll stop and if. But Christ, there couldn't be! "I don't think there was anyone there."

"But, for heaven's . . ."

"Just a minute, just a. I know what you're going to say. What if there is, eh? What if there is. Well." Aha, he's stopped, and that makes it easier, oh boy! "Well if there is, and anything can be done, then." The coup de grace, here's the coup. "That car behind will do it." In astonishment they turn as I explain in my thought-out voice hah! Reasonable man is the one who overcomes, the well-considered, thoughtful man. "And the best thing we can do is, well, you know. Get straight into town and report everything to the proper authorities; alert the police, the ambulance."

"What if the guy's dying or something, what if he's really in bad shape?" Unpleasant. A thought. Good Lord. Private dying noises; crying, crying out from his no-man's land and we'd have to watch or wipe the blood from his broken mouth. Jesus arrgh! Terrible. "I dunno, I certainly think we should have." Backwards staring, tentative and; expansive Lucan, I think you've won, you well-considered man but then he, don't for, please my head! Slapping angrily the seat's back, suddenly there's spittle, his lousy spittle for chrissakes spewing on my ears! "Goddamnit! You can't, you can't just drive by a thing like that without a look, without even looking at him for chrissakes! May be bleeding, may be bleeding to death and all he needs is a tourniquet, or something; maybe he." Jeez, what a sensationalist!

"C'om Oswald. Take hold of yourself, for heaven's sake young man. Take hold. You're blowing this, why you're. Blowing this out of all proportion." Tried, exasperated Lucan for I've tried, God knows I've. "Explained it to you, very clearly I thought. And I'll say it. Again. Best thing we can do. For speed." Very patient, very clear and patient, that's the thing. "Is drive on into town and. Notify the authorities." Boy, doesn't he know. Anything? Amateurs can't just go dragging the gravely injured around, you know. Do great damage, irreparable internal damage, joggle and twist all sorts of things out of place you know, so even if there were someone. Which I seriously doubt. We couldn't have moved him anyway, could we?" That's perfectly clear, and. Crawling in there to pull him out, God knows what harm we might have done. "If it's just a matter of. First Aid. Well, well the car behind will."

"I'm sorry. I'm sorry Doctor Crackell but that doesn't." Interrupting, he's continually interrupting and we'll have to have a. Talk. "It doesn't satisfy me. We should have . . ."

"Doesn't what? Doesn't satisfy? Look Oswald, I don't care if it satisfies you or not!" Jeez the nerve, the! We'll straighten this out once and for all, yes we. "I'm not one of your, your." Scathing. My best and biting scathing voice, arrogant punk, he has to learn. "Friends. You forget who you're talking to, I'm . . ."

"I know exactly who I'm talking to, and I'm sorry, but." Thunderstruck and God there's going to be. "But it bloody well makes me sick; driving away, away from." Don't want a. Scene. Good Lord! I'm just not up to that, my head and my poor sad nerves are not. I've got enough. Lucan's icy voice in the driving snow and Stratford now below that hill.

"We won't discuss this any more at the moment Oswald." Sternly, quickly, for I must strike fear, I must! Or. "When we return to the university, this whole matter will deserve, deserve a thorough examination." Ominously said, that's the thing, cow him into. Silence. "However. I don't wish to discuss it any further here. It's not appropriate."

"We didn't know there was another car, we had no way." Stop him! Raising hand, abruptly from the wheel.

"That's enough, I said! I refuse to listen or discuss." Girls' silence, awkwardness and Christ. This memory haunted landscape! And I didn't handle that well.

Rushing the crest of this last small hill and there, there! Burning wind, shrouded water tower; clumsy gate on the town's near edge. You're such a fraud Lucan, such a pompous fraud! Under the tree-top eaves, laughter and her body thick, fullskirted with my child; biting laughter and the sun. Hot on the shabby trunks. You talk about the book, but you're afraid! Come with me. Wooing. Come away, oh Lucan why don't you come with me! And I can't, I. Can't. Bewildered and frightened, his back to the room he stares on the street below. Why won't she? Marry me, even now, why won't she marry me and come to London, good job. I have a position waiting there. Folding behind me, stripping our rooms and folding. Packing, she's packing one by one the. Can't just! Oh God, she mustn't just go sailing off alone, pregnant and alone to have my baby in a strange town. She. Goddamnit Vera, turning desperately, you can't go off alone like this, you simply can't! In a strange town.

Then you'll have to come with me, won't you? Smiling, her voice and gentle. Or else I'll have to find someone else. What kind of? This, at a time like. Facetiousness is out of place and a tiny life is at stake. Helpless in her eyes; I must be. Firm. She's so frigging unrealistic! Wow! Can't go, go running off to England after her, so. Firmness, masculine perogative. To assert the. But she went anyway, she just. Scattered redbrick boxes, ugly in the grimy snow and makeshift factories' concrete blocks; not a full grown tree, the builders root them all up and she went without phoning or anything. Just a letter and I. Terrible bloody position to be in. Christ! I did everything I.

Could have, if she wanted to she could have married! Me. Moisture on these palms, handrubbing energetically; one and then the other. Wrote her too, I tried to help. Twice she. Blown mound, the service station there with shadowed pumps and lonely swinging washed-out lights; houses, of course the town has grown we all, weallhaveallhavealland I'm not anymore. Good Lord, that boy! Snow wild night, crisp underfoot with burning circles round my legs; young man a foolish, acid in my throat, I walked all night and self-afraid. Harsh weight upon me while dark birds drift and swayed; under eyes I've run, impatient voices crying in my ears like bees, suck, suck as the hands reached out and I. HAVE WANTED SO MUCH! Are you happy here? Rampant snowy road, obscured the view and trembling Lucan staring cry-filled, plump and hopeless at that boy who, panicking, vanished under this bridge and down the never ending hill. Reaching hands to the cross; reaching to smoothe, on the hill, read the reluctant paper crackling on its chest. Cavernous lie! Unhealthy minds, for. Wilful obscenity, a vulgar prank and it's clear that. That each day breaks newly born or. At least. At least the possibility, there has to be that, the possibility! For once, singing I. Danced around. These streets! A dancer. Gloomy on fire these stores, the tannery they've all come home in reflected light and Lucan's falling, falling in the long hall, precipitously falling and he peels away like pages blowing in the wind. Lousy lie, it's all a lousy lie! This trip and all, this fuckingawful drive and on and on I'll go forever hopeless down this filthy road. And as to, to what is anguish in me. Boy! She hasn't a, not a fucking clue as on and on. Have wanted so. But sickness, always wanting is the constant now and always, God! What am I to do, what hope for years or my life? What is there to do in fact (and the words in isolation clearly sound), what is there for me to do between the funeral and. The other? Not a prayer! Surrounding, the silence; and the answer's too well known, dear. Blessed. Heaven. Alone, sometimes and inescapable the answer that sickening, drags a question through my life. Nothing. Nothing. Can with the rest of. Happy? The hill and phoney. Nothing. To do and it doesn't. "There's the police station." Matter. What? Christ I hate that voice, I hate. Groping for, Lucan searching for the implication of. Yes, yes. The wreck and

I mustn't, the wreck dear God and I mustn't let him see it slipped my. Mind.

"Ah yes, I know, I know but." Surely. There couldn't have been! Surely, surely they're. "Since we're behind schedule, I've decided to, to phone." Pretty lame, that's hardly good, but. What's that, a groan, did he? Bastard, the. Forcefully, take control for pity's sake, assert. "We'll phone from the restaurant!" What else can I? Can't let him see. Terrible fool if we went in there and the, the crash was old or something, feel a terrible. "No need is there, to get involved or. When a phone call's good. Enough." I'm flushing, again, I'm, angry for why am I? Here I am again. "There'd be questions, signing papers maybe." Bloody inquisition and I swallow, every bloody time I. Useless argument and I'm so defensive with this miserable, this prick. Jeez!

"Let me out!" Startled Lucan turning, swerving startled on the road. "Stop the car and let me out." Staring, his eyes and angry into mine. Despising me. And reflexively back to see in this lousy town, breaking, to the roadside carefully. And icy wind through the door.

"Be a pleasure. If you feel." This way, oh God! So sick and overwhelmed, so helpless a bloody pawn, I am. Slamming cold behind me as he goes. For I'm defensive, bound about by. Forcing me, that's it, they're always. Putting me on the frigging spot and it's all a hoax, a stinking fraud! Accelerating from the curb and I see it so clearly, so inescapably; how could I? On his side, they're loathing, despising me too. No, no! "Don't know why he's so upset." Ease their awkwardness and I must. "A phone call would have done the trick just as easily." Embarrassment at these grasping hopes, my poor life's futility, for all along they've simply. USED CARS. USED CARS. Above and reaching alone through the tearing sky an iron pole bedecked; torn plastic pennants gusting down to the lot's four corners there. SAVE! Huge clumsy lettered on this vastly wasted, broken carousel. DIFFERENT. DIFFERENT. DIFFERENT. In price . . . in trade-in . . . How could I have. Believed, how could I? SAVE oh save me for I do. NOBODY EVER WALKS AWAY FROM HERE!!! Repent, I do dear God oh. SAVE! SAVE! Suddenly, violently. Horribly sick all over the floor oh. Terrible, the shameful scene, this growing stain of my youth and I did I sent her money, twice I sent. But she returned it. Everytime she. Have to get someone. Private, her life alone, gone with her own life somewhere and the child. Why did she, that's what I want to; why did she send it? Back. Why? Dirtworn above chrome and bright stores, this winter-landscaped mainstreet town: clumsy figures bundling lonely in the snow, burning the sound and sight of this past and underworld terrain. Almost nine, boy or girl of almost nine what kind of a life for a boy. Or girl. What kind of a life for her? Young, my figure walking still and driven the snow-filled streets: alone and away all walking dark and huddled here. Howling the night's white noise.

RAY SMITH 1941–

Ray Smith (b. Mabou, NS) has published several novels, including *Lord Nelson Tavern* (1974), *Century* (1986), and *The Man Who Loved Jane Austen* (1999). Smith won the QSPELL Hugh MacLennan Award for his farce, *A Night at the Opera* (1992). He has taught English at Dawson College in Montreal since 1968. He has suggested that, because "[a] story moves by its own rules . . . which are often not clear, even to the writer, until after the story is done," writers must feel free to explore other more abstruse features of narration (including, for example, the use of semicolons): "[t]here is no law that a story must have a plot."[5] His eccentric anecdotes often disrupt the unities of realism by placing idiosyncratic characters in totally anachronistic situations.

"Raphael Anachronic" first appears in *Cape Breton is the Thought-Control Centre of Canada* (1969), an anthology of comic tales lampooning the official literary standards that often derogate unusual regional writing in Canada. Just as Raphael in his fresco *School of Athens* might indulge in anachronism by depicting himself fraternizing with the philosophers of classical antiquity, so also has Smith depicted Raphael in an updated, rather than ancient, context, transplanting the maestro into the supercilious, cosmopolitan world of contemporary, experimental art. Such a macaronic biography illustrates how postmodernity can dehistoricize a specific artistic period, like the Renaissance, and then contextualize it within a "now" that juxtaposes and interfuses completely dissimilar styles.

"RAPHAEL ANACHRONIC" FROM *CAPE BRETON IS THE THOUGHT-CONTROL CENTRE OF CANADA*
BY RAY SMITH

HIS RIVALS

"LEONARDO," said handsome young Raphaello Santi, "What is Leonardo?"

His mistress Lucia said nothing, for the painter only asked questions of himself, and then only questions for which he already had the answer. Lucia had understood this as soon as she met him. She would probably remain his mistress for at least a month.

She said nothing; she refilled his glass with scotch.

"Leonardo is a scientist with a good pencil sharpener. He has a great future . . . programming computers."

"Yes master."

"Yes master," he parodied.

Raphael saw himself as a great wit. He had been polishing that Leonardo cut for six weeks. Lucia was the fifth mistress to have heard it. Raphael had another for Michelangelo: "A great feeling for form has Buonarotti. A great feeling for sculptural effects. With practice he might become a first rate cartoonist for the sports pages."

"And what of Botticelli, master?"

"Belt up, you silly twit; I ask the questions around here."

A DAY WITH RAPHAEL

It could not be said of Raphael that he was not a hard worker, no indeed! After nights of wine, song and amorous escapade (of reading himself to sleep with Vasari or Walter Pater) the young master would be demanding coffee and croissants from his mistress at eight sharp. He had an expensive Swiss alarm clock. An hour of primping and he was off to the studio or wherever he happened to be doing a fresco just then for he did a lot of frescoes among other things. He also did 5BX in the morning for his figure. He worked until teatime.

Raphael would begin the evening at a bar near work. People gathered to pay court. Raphael would say:

"Dali has a facile touch with a brush. He would do well illustrating medical textbooks."

But Raphael did not love the grovellers; he tired of their agreement, saying:

"Of course I am a well-rounded Renaissance man. I am great at everything. I only paint for money. Money you need to keep the little ladies happy."

Then he would grab his mistress obscenely and everyone would laugh. Disgusting.

RAPHAEL AT THE MUSEUM

In a museum one afternoon, Raphael exhibited to a Japanese mistress he had just then that he was a well-rounded Renaissance man. (This was one of his favorite motifs: "After crossing the stony desert of the Dark Ages, Man comes at last to the lush garden of the Renaissance; at the center of that garden is a flower of celestial loveliness; that flower is me.") He went about with a clipboard and wrote down the generic names of all the fossils.

"Walter Pater calls me a scholar," he said.

The Japanese girl was not at all impressed; she was interested only in social formalities. She was very patient, however.

"Now the Jurassic period was a great age," he declared. He then translated the Latin names of the fossils. He had a most limited knowledge of Latin; he bulled through; he could see nothing wrong in this.

"Yes, and so was the Cretaceous, hmm, hmmm."

RAPHAEL MEETS THE HIPPIES

One night, while strolling with his boringly madonna-like mistress Paola, Raphael came upon some hippies. His own hair was far below his shoulders so he did not comment upon the hippies' hair. Instead, he said:

"Hey, you."

"Yes?"

"Do you smoke pot?"

"No," they replied with predictable caution.

"I do," said a girl hippie.

"Wait here, Paola," Raphael whispered. "What I have to say is not for your delicate ears." Then Raphael gave the girl hippie a lecture on virtue, beauty and truth. The hippies nodded their heads enthusiastically. Raphael concluded:

"Furthermore, if you are to be of any use to the world or yourselves, I would suggest you find an occupation appropriate to your talents and constructive to society. . . . Like ditchdigging."

Raphael had a lot of snappy remarks like that one.

RAPHAEL FIGHTS WITH TWO MISTRESSES

Raphael only ever had one Russian mistress. She was a third generation emigrée, and very high strung. Her name was Galina. One night, in hopes of getting to the opera on time, Galina said:

"Raphael darling, I do so loathe missing the whole first act. Would you hurry with your perfume."

Raphael threw her out at once.

"Asian blood," he said. "Paugh!"

Another time Raphael got himself mixed up with a Scandinavian girl named Sigrid. He had a fight with her and she flattened him. It was not that Raphael was afraid to hit a woman, but that he incautiously hit the wrong one. Raphael dearly wished to brag about his physical prowess.

RAPHAEL FLIES IN AN AIRPLANE

On the invitation of a prestigious gallery, Raphael once agreed to fly to another city for an opening. His mistress, Sophia, came along to soothe him and to handle the excess-baggage bankroll.

"My, what a lovely airport," said Sophia.

This infuriated Raphael. The airport was filthy, the other passengers common, the airplane had been invented by DaVinci and would therefore not work.

But the stewardess sweet-talked him and Sophia caressed him and at last he agreed to mount the ramp.

"The *Times*," he demanded in a stage-English accent. "I want my *Times*."

Sophia had been briefed on the *Times*; she flourished it. For Raphael considered Englishmen the only true travellers and when travelling endeavoured always to pass for one. He was dressed in tweeds, with a tweed cloth cap and sat sweltering under a massive tweed blanket. But his patent leather pointy-toed shoes gave him away.

"Don't let him worry you," Sophia lied to the stewardess, "He's allergic to aluminum."

"Alu*mini*um," Raphael corrected.

Airborne, he scoffed at the sky, utterly blue above the clouds. "Painted better skies at the age of three. Nature: Bah! Humbug!"

He visited the toilet eight times in the belief that he was defecating directly onto the farmers far below. After each flush he would hiss, "Peasants," into the hole.

RAPHAEL A COMMANDO

During the war, Raphael distinguished himself with the commandos. He even got the M.C. In his eyes this vindicated the statement he had made to the sergeant-major at the recruiting depot:

"Virtue is the basis of all action. I am the world's greatest painter; this requires the greatest virtue; I will therefore be the world's greatest soldier."

He also explained his greatness in these terms to his many wartime mistresses.

If the truth be known, Raphael did very well for a cream puff.

(If the truth be known, Raphael was not in England at all during the war, for he held an Italian passport and would have been interned for the duration.)

RAPHAEL A FINANCIER

In his studio, along with the paraphernalia of his trade, Raphael kept an old peanut butter jar with a slit in the lid. Into this he put at the end of each day all his pennies.

"How practical you are, Raphael," commented his English mistress, Penelope.

"Of course. An artist is essentially the most practical of types."

She effused upon this subject until Raphael realized she thought he was saving for a rainy day.

"Of course not, you nit, I'm going to corner the market in copper."

Nevertheless, he did not throw her out just then, but a few days later in an argument over central heating.

RAPHAEL WATCHES TELEVISION

The only television programmes Raphael could abide were the spear-and-sandal late shows. He was not impressed by the technology ("A DaVincian trick") and not unreasonably claimed he could paint better pictures with his eyes closed. All sitcoms he found idiotic; features he reviled for they were not about him.

But once the conventions of the medium had been explained to him, Raphael could watch such things as "Hannibal and the Elephant-girl" or "The Sword of Tacitus" with quivering delight.

When the triumphant gladiator had his opponent at his mercy and was looking to Nero for a sign, Raphael would cry: "He deserves an honourable death!" and with a look of respect on his weasly face Nero would turn his thumb down.

"Bravo! Bravo!"

Raphael thought Nero had taken his advice; that's how naive he was.

RAPHAEL MEETS ANDREW WYETH

Raphael once condescended to go to Chadd's Ford to visit Andrew Wyeth. They got on because Raphael did most of the talking. So long as he stuck to subjects like the superiority of hand-ground pigments, everything was fine. In the evenings they reminisced:

> *Raphael:* Things were different in the old days. . . .
>
> *Wyeth:* Perhaps you knew my father . . . he died tragically in a train wreck. . . .
>
> *Raphael:* No, it couldn't have been in my time . . . the trains were pretty slow in Urbino back then. . . . (Thinks: what a simpleton!)

After a week, though, the differences came out. In the face of such self-assured technical mastery, Raphael felt compelled to bruit about his own talent and charm. He got onto subject matter: "Magnitude . . . sublimity . . ." he declared.

Wyeth threw him out; besides he had been leaving cigar ashes all over.

HIS ARROGANCE

Raphael, the entire world acknowledges your genius; why then are you so arrogant?

This was said by Vera, the most perceptive mistress Raphael ever tolerated.

Raphael stopped his scotch glass halfway to his lips. Vera waited quietly. After a while Raphael said:

"I don't know, Vera."

She wondered if it was just his being Italian; did other Italians brag? It was certainly an accepted cliché. Well, yes, he thought it might be so, but then no Italian had so much to brag about as he. After all. . . .

"Perhaps it's the old story about the alienation of the artist. . . ."

"Bunk!" exclaimed Raphael. He was *quattro-cento*; alienation was nonsense. Artists were greater than anyone else, thus the least alienated; the sergeant-major is never out of step.

Later that afternoon Raphael got a call from the Vatican. Leo X wanted another painting.

"Oh boy, oh boy, oh boy!" cried Raphael. "I'll slap off another madonna for him tomorrow afternoon and really soak him for it. These popes are filthy rich."

He took Vera right downtown and bought himself a dove-grey Ferrari with four on the floor. Raphael knew what was what.

HIS DEATH

Of course, Raphael claimed mastery of all sports; but being a canny fellow with much of his time taken up with work, women and cocktail parties, people found it difficult to put his boast to the test.

Spectator sports offered Raphael a neat compromise. He went with Sandy to a baseball game and with Francesca to a soccer match. He would criticize the players with impunity. But he said: "I do not see the point of watching sports. Surely this is absurd. Especially for me, for I am better by far than these professional hacks."

Also, he said of the crowds: "Rabble."

An English mistress, Cynthia, got him to play a round of golf with her. But he so praised his own play and so ridiculed hers (she was, in fact, quite good) that she stomped off after the ninth hole.

"A product of inferior breeding," Raphael shrugged.

Raphael continued on his own, much puffed up. No one could now question his eccentric method of scoring which was: he would survey the hole from the tee, estimate his desired play, score same, then tee off. So confident was he that he followed a vicious hook into a swamp. He hacked and splashed at the ball for half an hour saying, "That didn't count . . . that didn't count . . ." and then went home with pneumonia and so died.

He was later reported by at least four golfers to have been seen improving his lie.

RAPHAEL: THE CONSIDERED CRITICAL OPINION

When all was said and done the critics decided this: Raphael was a pretty obnoxious guy, but he sure could paint madonnas.

MICHAEL ONDAATJE 1943–

Michael Ondaatje (b. Colombo, Sri Lanka) has published numerous books of poetry, including *The Dainty Monsters* (1967), *The Man With Seven Toes* (1969), *Rat Jelly* (1973), *Secular Love* (1984), and *Handwriting* (1998). His novels include *Coming Through Slaughter* (1976), *Running in the Family* (1982), and *In the Skin of a Lion* (1987). He has won the Governor General's Award four times: twice for poetry, with *The Collected Works of Billy the Kid* (1970) and *There's a Trick with a Knife I'm Learning To Do* (1979); and twice for fiction, with *The English Patient* (1992) and *Anil's Ghost* (2000). He has also won the Booker Prize for *The English Patient*, and the cinematic treatment of this novel won an Academy Award for Best Picture (1996).

"Billy the Kid and the Princess" constitutes one of the most interesting sustained examples of a "found story" in Canadian literature, since the text quotes, verbatim, the complete dialogue from a comic book. Stephen Scobie suggests that, for a popular culture in which every historical figure must become a mythomanic legend, this fairytale represents "Billy's apotheosis."[6] Like the found poems of Bern Porter, who discovers pop art in discarded pamphlets, this story by Ondaatje suggests that plagiarism itself constitutes an outlawed, literary version of the "readymade," formulated by Marcel Duchamp (whose artwork often consists of a prefabricated item, like a bottlerack, purchased from a market and then exhibited in a museum).

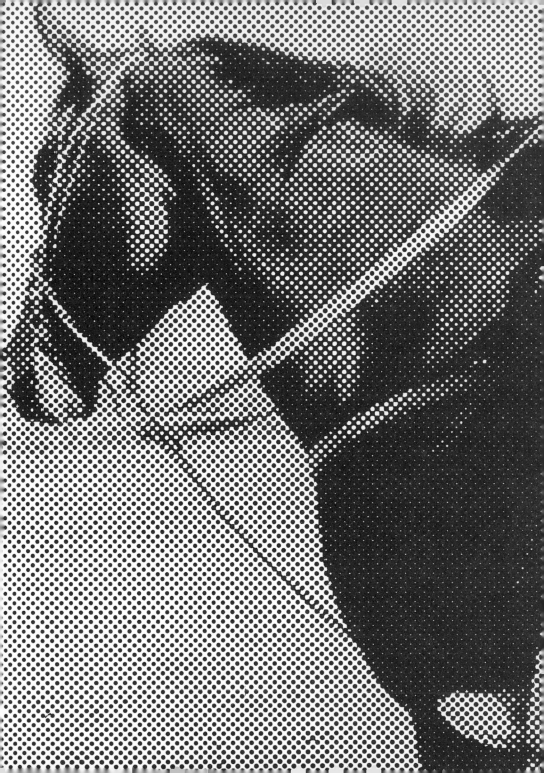

"BILLY THE KID AND THE PRINCESS" FROM
THE COLLECTED WORKS OF BILLY THE KID
BY MICHAEL ONDAATJE

THE Castel of the Spanish girl called "La Princesa" towered above the broad fertile valley . . . in the looming hills there were gold and silver mines . . . Truly, the man chosen to rule beside the loveliest woman in Mexico would be a king. The girl had chosen William H. Bonney to reign with her . . . but a massive brute named Toro Cuneo craved that honor . . .

There's been a cattle war in Jackson Country . . . He'd settled a beef with three gunquick brothers near Tucson . . . and he was weary of gunthunder and sudden death! Billy the Kid turned his cayuse south . . . splashed across the drought dried Rio Grande . . . and let the sun bake the tension out of his mind and body.

"See them sawtooth peaks, Caballo? There's a little town yonder with a real cold cerveza and a fat lady who can cook Mexican food better'n anybody in the world! This lady also got a daughter . . . una muchacho . . . who's got shinin' black hair and a gleam in her brown eyes I want to see again."

And on a distant hill . . .
"He comes, be ready Soto."

"Gunshots . . . a 45 pistol! Runaway! It's a girl! She's goin' to take a spill! Faster Chico!"

"AAAAAHH!"

"Hang on . . . I got yuh! . . . You're okay now Señorita."

"Gracias, Señor. You are so strong and brave . . . and very gallant!"

"Thanks, I heard shots . . . Did they scare your cayuse into runnin' away?"

"I think I can stand now, Señor . . . if you will put me down."

"Huh? Oh sorry, Señorita. I'm Billy Bonney, Señorita. I'm from up around Tucson."

"I am Marguerita Juliana de Guelva y Solanza, la Princesa de Guelva."

"La Princesa? A *real* princess?"

"I am direct descendent of King Phillip of Spain. By virtue of Royal land grants, I own this land west for 200 leagues, south for 180 leagues. It is as large as some European kingdoms . . . larger than two of your American states . . . I am still a little weak. Ride with me to the castle, Señor Bonney."

"*There* Señor Bonney . . . my ancestral home. The castle and the valley farther than you can see . . . I have 20,000 cattle, almost as many horses and herds of goats, pigs, chickens. Everything my people need to live."

"WHOOOEEE! The Governor's mansion up at Phoenix would fit in one end o' that wickiup."

"Come on, Yanqui! It is late . . . you must have dinner with me."

"ATTENTION! HER EXCELLENCY RETURNS!"

Thinks: "She's got a regular army!"

The man called Billy the Kid is not impressed by the magnificent richness of his surroundings. The golden cutlery means nothing . . . The priceless china and crystal matter not, and the food cooked by a French chef? — PFAAGGH!

Thinks: "I'd sooner be in Mama Rosa's kitchen eatin' tortillas an' chile with Rosita battin' them dark eyes at me!"

"This table needs a man like you, Señor Bonney. Others have occupied that chair but none so well as you."

"Gracias, Princesa . . . but I'd never feel right in it . . . if you know what I mean."

"I propose a toast, my gringo friend . . . to our meeting . . . to your gallant rescue of me!"

"I reckon I can't let a lady drink alone, Princesa."

CRASH!!!

"He could have sunk it in my neck just as easy . . . Start talkin' hombre 'fore I say *my* piece about that knife throwing act!"

"I am a man of action, not words, gringo! I weel crack your ribs . . . break your wrists . . . then send you back where you belong!"

"Come on, animal, I want to finish dinner!"

SOCK! !

Thinks: "If I can nail him quick I'll take the fight out of him . . . PERFECT!"

That was his Sunday punch . . . and Toro laughed at it! Now, Billy the Kid knows he's in for a struggle!

"He's got a granite jaw which means . . . I'll have to weaken him with powerful hooks to the stomach! OOoowww!" THUD!

"Now it's my turn!"

"If he lays a hand on me . . ."

SWISSS!

SOCK!

"I keel you gringo!"

Thinks: "My head . . . he busted my jaw!"

TOCK!

Thinks: "He's a stomper . . ."

"I keel your pet gringo Excellencia!"

"Yuh'll take me tuh death maybe, hombre!"

"You no escape Toro now!"
"I didn't figure on escapin' Toro!"
CRACK!
"Over you go, Toro!" "Olé! Olé!"
CRASH

"Sorry I busted the place up some, Princesa."

"You are mucho hombre, Yanqui, very much man! A man like you could help me rule this wild kingdom! Will you remain as my guest for a time?"

"I come down here to rest up some. I reckon I can do that here as well as in Mama Rosa's cantina."

(Kiss)

"That was to thank you for protecting me from Toro Cueno. I must not go on being formal with you . . ."

In the next few days, Billy the Kid was with La Princesa often.

Long rides through wild country . . .

"Wait princess . . . don't get ahead of me!"

"EEEEEeeii! !"

"Duck, princess!"

BANG! BANG!

"Once more Chivoto, you have saved my life, this time from that cougar. You have won my love!"

"Hold on, ma'am . . ."

Before Billy the Kid can defend himself, La Princesa Marguerita has taken him in her arms and. . . .

CHRIS SCOTT 1945–

Chris Scott (b. Hull, England) has published several books of fiction, including *Bartleby* (1971), *To Catch a Spy* (1978), and *Hitler's Bomb* (1984). His novel *Antichthon* (1982), about the life of Giordano Bruno, was nominated for the Governor General's Award, and his novel *Jack* (1988), about the life of Jack the Ripper, won the Arthur Ellis Award. He was a Fulbright Scholar at Pennsylvania State University (1968), and has taught creative writing at campuses around Lake Superior. He has also written many reviews for *Books in Canada* (1972–1978). He has worked as a farmer, raising cattle and horses in the Ottawa Valley, and he presently lives on an island in northern Ontario.

Bartleby is a meandering, picaresque adventure written with the same ironic spirit found in *Tristram Shandy*, by Lawrence Sterne. Scott attempts to recount the biography of a character called Bartleby, but in doing so, Scott does little more than recount the hardships of composing a narrative called *Bartleby*. W. H. New has remarked that "Scott contrives to write about . . . Writing" in a kind a "funhouse," where an author loses control of his characters, all of whom quarrel with the designs of their creator.[7] The first chapter provides a parodic apology for the license taken by the author, who has seen fit to defy the traditional conventions of narrative, thereby earning the condemnation of a critic, who nevertheless offers recommendations for improving the work.

FROM *BARTLEBY*
BY CHRIS SCOTT

*An Apology of Apologies, Wherein a Would-Be Bard Sets Forth His
Reasons for Writing Such a Book at Such a Time, and Possessed by a
Sense of Redundancy, Is Constrained to Apologize for Writing a Book
at All — or No Book.*

HEAVENLY reader, let me anticipate your two most serious objections to
Bartleby: the first that it is a work of plagiarism; the second that it employs
too many gimmicks, stocks in trade, and clichés of the writer's imitative art.
You say Bartleby is no fit name for a hero, for it has been used by the incom-
parable Melville. Then, yes, candidly I admit I have stolen the name though
not its character, who seemed to me a dead man from the start. Or rather *I*
have not stolen the name, but come by it, expropriated it, in what manner and
wise you will presently see.

I like the sound *Bartleby*. In so far as it has certain memorable associ-
ations, it has put me in the way of writing a novel without actually having to
go to such lengths, hence placing, or appearing to place me within a tradition
we moderns lack. Should the hero have been called, *V*, *W*, *X*, *Y*, or for that
matter, *Z*, or should he have remained nameless, the device would have been
a mere concession to the rabblement's taste. As for the accusation of plagiarism, a charge subsequently put around in this text by a character other than
the hero, it is acceptable, even welcome to me. For now all things are writ
large and apocalyptically, and the world outside the poor writer's playroom

falls into little pieces, what does he have at hand but an abacus of sorts, whereon to spell out — as best he can — the words Alpha and Omega? Let other bards plagiarize life; I have plagiarized a book.

Your second objection, I must admit, is more perplexing than the first. This very apology might appear as no more than a gimmick which — I hasten to assure you — was not at all in my mind when *Bartleby* came my way and I was on relatively easier terms with the world and myself. In those days I had projected an essay of my own: a very moral work to set this present age aright, a novelist's novel that would restore the harmonious principles of nice observation and just portraiture, in modern times usurped by the disfigured and grotesque minions of Dulness. Indeed I had actually compiled three or four chapters, scribblings — alas! — occupying more time and space in the drawer of my desk and the ambitions of its owner than in the critical light of day, to which, had they been exposed (as they eventually were), they would have amounted to less than nothing (as they eventually did).

Then — from this author of nothing at all — enough is said if I tell you that midway in time and place of my efforts as a would-be bard, with my hero still unchristened, a terrible uncertainty fell upon me, drying up the ink in my pen and, almost, the blood in my veins.

For there I was (and am) in a country where a certain prophet had been sown and reaped; a visionary in whose hallowed and harrowing wake bards trembled and bards fell. Here I was scratching out a tenanted life in the very city where this seer uttered utterances, said sayings, saw seeings, and see-sawed; here I was at the third remove of my life where the earth was barren, the seed blighted, the air unpropitious, the climate not conducive to bardic endeavours such as mine.

What gentle madness can have possessed me?

But I had a friend, a fantastical rococo friend, to whom in a fit of the *furor scribendi* I had loaned my pages. What would he say? Would he recognize my art; give me praise, encouragement, *flattery*? Or would my script be condemned to oblivion; my hero damned, given not even the best room in hell, though unbaptized?

We discoursed in generalities, my friend and I, until I raised those very infelicities and inadequacies, attributes of would-being and death, with which this apology has so far belaboured the reader. Yet I also propounded the strengths of my work, my *Autobiography of a Dead Man*. Was this not a novel idea for a book, an unprecedented idea, nothing less than a stroke of genius in fact: the idea of a sleeping hero — a hero who, although he walked and talked, drank and defecated, although he was seemingly awake — was actually *asleep*, and, asleep, *dead*? What forms there were to be explored! What an autopsy might be performed as my hero was laid out, cut open, and stitched up with incisive precision! Surely this was a revolutionary work!

This was my friend's reply — friend, do I say?

"Your intended work has nothing to commend it to the tribunal of popular taste at whose bar, if you wish for success, it must receive infallible judgement. Here is no *Sturm und Drang* of the *American* School: none of the Hebraic complaints and laments of Wrath, nor the existential pugilism of Rojack, nor the cybernetic trickery and borrowed cadences of Johannes Carp. Neither the corncobs and rhetoric of the great tradition, nor the lasciviousness and inguinal feats of the new, grace the pages you have shown me. As for the ontological concern and the leaping into and out of being of the *French* School, I here discern no monocles, autodidacts, plagues, windows on the world, no epistemologically multitudinous polysyllables to baffle the reader (your judge) and draw his applause. The word *Angst* is apparently unknown to you; self-searchings, *crises d'identité*, and dark nights of the human soul — asleep or otherwise — haunt none of your chapters. Why, where the *Germans* are concerned you seem merely untutored: grim drolleries, theatres of life (and death), blood cults, maniacal pacts, Weimar's perfect constitution, goblins, the sublimely demonic, will never keep your readers from their beds on a windy night. Furthermore, *Russian* buffoonery, grotesqueries, simpletons, idiots, horses, drunkards, wars, revolutions, assassinations, in short that heightened verisimilitude of the underground and ground-under writer which would have won you the deserved title, plagiarist and *bard*, all these you have most carelessly omitted. I would think you totally

unacquainted, moreover, with the *English* stable of feminine delights —
Lesser, Flame, Frigid Trophy, and Victoria Prickens — were it not for the
fact that you have confessed the many edifying and pleasurable hours you
have spent perusing their voluminous productions. Yet neither lesbian house-
wives nor bawdy curates appear in your pages to delight the ingenuous and
make the spinster leave off her knitting. And most unhappy criticism of all:
those *Irish* flights of Sorrow, in whichever guise he chose to appear, whether
as Windbreak or Belch where the Liffey flows from its sump unconscious,
this SORROW, progenitor of the Fluvial Tradition and father of us all, trick-
les but thinly through your work — though his influence, I grant you, is made
everywhere present by its conspicuous absence."

My friend was reminded that the book was incomplete. But my face
must have portrayed my disappointment, for he continued:

"Incomplete? That is hardly the word for it. However, concerning this
very absence of content, this vacuity which I have critically touched upon,
such inanity seems to me a recommendation — especially in this day and age
— rather than the condemnation which you seem to think it. For, inasmuch
as the silent symphony, the wordless language, the invisible portrait are in
great contemporary demand and loom under the general and compendious
term symbolic, so too will your work, when finished after the method I have
in mind, gain easy acceptance with the public. Which body and its shepherd,
the critic, rejoice in such emptiness and proceed under the following law:
that, if a work has something in it, they fall to contention and quarrelling
amongst themselves, and are full of envy and nastiness at seeing something
they have not themselves drawn up. Whereas if a work has nothing at all in
it, like yours, then they must of necessity perceive something in it to justify
their existence as critics, or more mundanely, in order to explain the time and
expense they have gone to in purchasing and reading nothing. Therefore it is
inevitable that your work will be acclaimed.

"However, I am troubled. In several, admittedly minor points of detail,
the piece may be accused of clarity. Your hero does not sufficiently assume the
role of anthropos and it would appear, by this, that you intend to demean

mankind. It is customary in this democratized age to emphasize what is known as the universality of human experience. Make your dead and sleeping heroic self speak for the entire species. You may think this egregious or patronizing, which indeed it is, but you must evoke the spirit of mass man, major man, man in his essential mediocrity, man as nothingness, before the witless public can be satisfied that something has, after all, happened.

He continued, "Upon the absence of plot, time, and locality, these features which you have taken as a disqualification are amongst the more noteworthy aspects of the piece, and it is this sequential confusion — whether you know it or not — that makes you worthy of the master, SORROW.

"Ah, but you claim you have written only one or two chapters; that plot and character and place have yet had no time to materialize. What, I ask, what of these unwritten chapters?"

"Well," I enquired, "what of them?"

"There's a terrible danger here," was the answer, "that your sleeping ambition may lure you into writing what is presently unwritten and unsaid. On the other hand, if you do not write them, if you leave them unwritten (as they already are), might you not be accused of writing nothing twice: thrice, in fact, for you have already left them unwritten, and not to write again would be to write the nothing that you have not written three times when once is enough.

"But not a whit! In these unwritten chapters — *left as they are* — you have actually achieved the impossible. Time in your invisible narrative — to pass lightly over but one of its inanities — is supplied by that infinite moment in which the Biscayan and Quixote are frozen in immortal combat, and in which we are left like Pierre Menard (capricious invention of that Argentinian whose name — like Poe before the Bostonians — temporarily escapes me), in which we, I say, are left to invent new Quixotes, to speculate on the course of the combat, to extrapolate, permutate, in short, surrender to a fiction. Hence, because of these very persuasive reasons, I take your unwritten chapters to be the best, the most accurate, the truest representation of your dead and sleeping hero's state of mind. They are without doubt infinitely more powerful than anything you have so far written."

Your apologist, meanwhile, was bereft of speech. In silence, I reflected, we have our beginning, and in silence our end. But what manner of work might approach this fantastic critic's requirements?

"In other respects," he continued, "I find the work wanting. To speak the truth, your work — finished or no — is but half of nothing rather than twice or thrice nothing, and lacks that apparency of something which the drowning reader might catch upon as a straw. Blind your average John Homer with the audacity of the lie: give him that straw and tell him it's a life-raft, and he will believe you.

"As for the rest, you must have pert introductions and witty colophons for the idle; asides, parodic forms, divertissements for the satirically bent; learning, scholarship, and the absence of all wisdom for the academic; parables for the wise; allegories for the pious, religion for the devout, symbols for fools; accident, contrivance, and the improbable for the speculative; design and inevitability for the determined; fair weather for the foul, and foul for the fair; revolution, reaction, and synthesis for the committed (as they call themselves) — above and beyond all for that ugly and impossible chimera, the public, you must unleash the great beast LIBIDO, and work it hard, as hard as you will, until your genius is acknowledged and the public satiated. Lastly, do not fail to address yourself to the troubles of this sorry world which some philosophers labour to prove does not exist, and still others to confute them; address yourself, I say, to the existent woes of this non-existent world — or *vice-versa* — in which task, as the author of a non-existent book, you have a marvellous competency."

I was much dismayed by this and declared my firm resolve to be an author no more. What little of the speech I could understand led me to believe that these were ill times for authors, even would-be authors, and that I would be well advised to abandon my ambitions and take honest employment as an honest man, content with obscurity.

"Nay, nay," declared my friend, "there are no honest men. But as for your resolution not to be an author, I wager you'll be one in spite of yourself, or more to the point, in spite of these unwritten chapters."

"How's that?" I asked, for despite my friend's commentary, there was something in me which still clamoured after bardship, something that would not be put down. "How might I be an author, if I have written less than half of nothing?"

"Because," said he, "I have the other half of less than half of nothing, or rather the whole of nothing."

"Come, come," said I, suspecting a joke at my expense, "what do you mean?"

"Simply that in all this I, your friend, have a friend — one other than you — who in his capacity as house spectre and public hack has already obliged, and gladly, with just such details as are called for. Voilà!" said he, producing that MS which has been, is, and shall always be, the occasion of my present woes, "these leaves, vaster by far than your own as the ocean is to a drop of water, you have but to variously interlard therein to be assured of a little space on posterity's boundless shores. Here — take them — and do what you will with them. For the presence or absence of your visible or invisible chapters will not be noticed here in this unwritten, written book."

So saying he bade farewell, leaving me not with one MS, but two.

How long ago this was, I do not *yet* care to tell, though I shall in due course. Whether this second book (a book without author, without plot, and for vast and heroically vacant sections, without Bartleby himself), whether it was the work of another's creation, or his own, got up and formed in another's image, I do not know. Nor can I even offer you assurance of this other's existence, except to say that I, more than my chapters, am a modest and unhappy proof of it.

For my friend, the fantastic, having prepared the way for Bartleby, has departed hence and taken leave of this terrestrial ball, never to appear again in the flesh until the twenty-second chapter of this history when your apologist was soundly berated for his treatment of the MS up to that time. I, in mid-passage, never did complete my work, but offer instead this cannibalized form, this illusion for which I disavow all responsibility, this mystic union of two souls: *myself* and *Bartleby*.

J. MICHAEL YATES 1938–

J. Michael Yates (b. Missouri, USA) is a founding editor of two presses: Sono Nis (1968) and Cacanadada (1989), both renowned for publishing unorthodox, surrealist literature by Canadians. Yates is a prolific producer of literature, and his numerous publications include *Man in the Glass Octopus* (1968), *The Great Bear Lake Meditations* (1970), *The Abstract Beast* (1972), *Breath of the Snow Leopard* (1974), *The Qualicum Physics* (1975), *Fazes in Elsewhen* (1976), *Fugue Brancusi* (1983), *The Completely Collapsible Portable Man* (1984), *Schedules of Silence* (1986), and *Line Screw* (1993). He is a winner of the Writer's Choice Award (1988). A former executive at the CBC, he has also worked at many universities as an instructor of creative writing.

"And Two Percent Zero" recounts the aqueous descent into madness of Max Higgins, a railroad engineer, who dies after serving for years as an industrial worker in an alpine wilderness. Yates has remarked that "[a] poet is a double-bladed cryptographer: from great enigmas, he burgles terror . . . then suffuses things commonplace with threat"[8] — hence, Yates writes an ominous, cryptic tale, whose oneiric imagery calls to mind the automatic scription of such surrealists as André Breton and Robert Desnos, both of whom explore the netherworld of unconscious compulsions by writing disparate, visionary sentences without any conscious, editorial intrusion. Like the flow of water that drowns the mind of the insane engineer, the flow of words threatens to drown the mind of the poetic narrator.

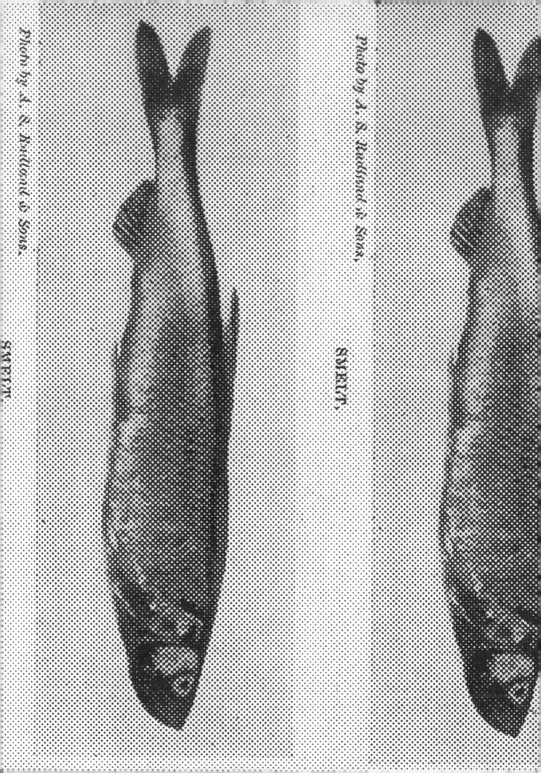

SPRATS.

Photo by F. N. Rutland & Sons.

SMELTS.

Photo by F. N. Rutland & Sons.

"AND TWO PERCENT ZERO"
FROM *THE ABSTRACT BEAST*
BY J. MICHAEL YATES

Dust. Surprisingly, we were all made of almost all water. Except for the dust. Beauty was water, brain was water, but something was always dust clinging to the shine of a piano-top and cataracting the windows.

THERE'S no question now whether I should protest this damming of the water. But even further stoppage of the current would be required to effect the objection. I would whisper to myself: you've left no channel unconsidered: things are as they are. But I would whisper back to me: stuff and ridiculous: if this is certain, how is it that you can even muster the moisture to doubt. Look at these interrogative tides. Be your own moon.

Drawn by no moon whatsoever, a tide is rising. Never will it recede. A small light of perception is staggering about the room perhaps two and a half feet above the carpet. Creases of trousers plunge from the chairs toward the floors like ravines in the peak-faces which vanish beneath the surfaces of fresh and salt water fjords. Ice nervously agitated in a glass. Something melting; something rising. The salal and teabush are drowning. A black bear lingers at the blueberries until his hind feet are under water, then winds off toward the outcroppings at the crest of a hogback ridge. Voice from above: Maximilian Higgins has become a tincture; they sent him to the hospital yesterday with wet brain. The idea, I say to myself, is to build the dam as high as I wish but leave a hole for the river to flow unimpeded through. The diminutive light collides with the corner of the coffee table. Flash of internal lights. Motes in the venetian rays through the salt water before the eyes. The worms drown by what then? to the surface of the mountain soil at the floors of my cells. The stuffed, glutted fish loging among them — sick fish, half dead from feeding, gills full of pine needles bits and mica dust. Deathly they shine when they breathe. Gastrula, blastula, the fistula of bog-water slowing to a flood. The small light steadies, the trouser-legs shorten, then grown torsos and heads. Taste of a drink much diluent from the single-minded capacity of the ice. The roof of an old and silvered cabin is floating, voyaging, nowhere. No hole in the concrete for the water to run through. Yes, I say, I know, and shape of the fluid mouthing up the slopes is snake, bird, fish, small boy with a beautiful blue lump on his forehead, outgrowing his clothing at an astounding rate. Ducks flying over circle several times, but the woodduck no longer recognizes the river stopped and circling upon itself behind the dam. Elsewhere. Elsewhere.

Coming-coming-coming three hootsfull into the sepia-blue morning, the steam whistle. Stop the water. All the water is leaking away. As you know, there's nothing I can do about the water. Keep your mind on what you're doing. If I turn on the radio, you won't hear the drip, but you know the noise of the announcers in the morning. The morning men. I'm all the morning man you can handle. Through the sharp elbows of warm pipe, the cool water goes, then blooms like a bombburst into the boiler. Parts of the universe begin to drive: stroke of a piston: the breath expels white into the willows at the railroad-side and a bull moose launches into the bog up to the wrists of his horns. Through the window, a dam under construction passes; the absent river has been diverted elsewhere. Children not allowed in the bar car where the hot hands of a young man are melting the ice in his glass. It was as if Max had been building up steam — stoking his own soul, just stoking and stoking — all his boyhood until he jubilantly drunk one night picked up the chain-saw and cut his house down from inside. His wife yelled something at him and he revved the saw at her. She went through a window and disappeared forever elsewhere. When the whole thing was in a heap there like a collapsed wooden lung, he set a match to it. Steam, I swear, not smoke, went up into the cavity the sky was that night. The needles in my cells are moving over the red-marks as I gaze at the creases of my trouser-legs. The snake with something to say says — disregard the burning bird and the fish that again flogs up your stream; the man stoking the boiler in the durable arctic light is soon going to hose the permafrost with steam and blade away the layers to the gold. Never trust man or mastadon who tampers with the ice.

I, with my bald head, extraordinary height, and size fourteen E feet, am about to refuse the dare to walk across the young ice of the old sewage plant. The cold is here, he hasn't drained his cells nor drunk enough electrolyte, and the afternoon will split him open like a water-pipe. Beneath the sky of ice the killer whales follow the shadow of a seal. The shadow of a man. Why not god? and this is beginning of the Tower of Babel Piscatorial. The host to him who tips the floe. Ice of my ice, the railroad's going viscous, that river of cargo, and a bull moose, in rut, head and railroad-catcher lowered, is steaming down the track toward the whistle. Let the faucet drip, the glaciers declare all the sea's a cocktail, and when they found Higgins frozen in his cabin, he was light as a cardboard box — from underneath the shrews had eaten away everything (bone, boots, britches) but the iced-up airward skin. Coal dust everywhere: he'd stoked his last ice-fog. There are no snakes here. The women have birds beneath their skirts. When you catch them through a hole, the fish flop about twice upon the ice and then freeze solid. You can't eat them. Possibly Higgins forgot that booze doesn't freeze solid, took a belt against the cold, and burned his life out with that gulp. The ice of the sewage plant is as ice as any other. We forget there's nothing to do with it — it under the ubiquitous ice.

There's knowledge in it, the way ice stops things the way a camera stops things and the alcohol does. But ice in the deep-freeze of memory simply goes off without melting. Sublime, just like that, and all he knows is that he no longer knows what he knew. The world is just a whistle-hoot in the cold distance and dangerous as a bear in a bad berry season. The railway snakes away into the blind white yonder, the heavy ravens rise slowly into the air full of rising ice, and the wind twists like a hooked fish down from the domes. Sublimely *blau* Maximilian's cells ascended with the ice, and Maximilian elected to follow the party.

Weather report: It's raining Maximilian Higgins all over the rainforest of her flesh; the deep green moss creeping out all her crevices has blurred her contiguations. They are, as it were, one fungus. His breath comes in short whistles, but the sound of drops falling drinks away all auditory distinctions. The mushrooms spring like short blasts of steam beneath the ferns. Rain brings down the dust, the mercuric pulver, the radioactive residue. Passengers on the train are wearing fish-bowls of water over their heads, but the smoke dissolved therein has given them all emphysema of the gills. Nevertheless, they are their diseases are travelling elsewhere, trouser-legs rain-drenched and wrinkled. The moon is melting in the celestial cocktail. Now that the secondary-growth fires have been extinguished in my cells, the erosion begins. So much of my hair and fingernails already in the sea.

The railroad on the seafloor excurses past the drill-shafts. Overhead the floating derricks bob like flower-blossoms in the wind. Maximilian Higgins is our smiling engineer. Three bulbous blasts on his small whistle, then a lubricious flit through the next and the next little mushroom of oil-cloud that exudes from the infinite orifices with which the Earth fornicates us one and all. It's not so good with the salt — like sand, so abrasive, it can injure us both. Let's go do it elsewhere. The water-birds are driving for small fish. The water-snakes prey upon the hungry birds. When the moon grew bored rising and falling the tides in my cells, it drew the water off the Earth and the sky was temporarily water-mottled. Dryness remained as a pair of empty trouser legs.

You calling to me through the fog in my finger-tips. I reply: moon-dust. You're thinking of the last street-signs and that there's no way here from anywhere, momentarily. And never was, Higgins hypothesizes, considering slow suicide by ice-fog. If the population and/or industry in this area increases by a factor of two, this will become a ghost-town. At first we swim through the cotton-candy weather which hovers over the ground at a thickness of six feet. Like fish. The gray residue seeps in the smallest crack, thickens upon the dash board, thickens upon the lungs. Like wingless birds, we leap straight up through the ice-fog to gasp in a little clear air. Like drowning heads about a drowning ship. Fog of my fog, the children go first, not tall enough for sustained leaping, then the women, then the shorter men. As the leaping grows more frenzied, the lungs collapse cauterized by the frozen air. Finally, even the basketball players who haven't to leap at all to breathe, even these must sit to rest or lie down to sleep. The weather in my cells will have me one way or another. I should like, at least, the winter arctic midday moon pursued by sundogs instead of this grained glass at the terminus of the long metabolic ceremony. Only the trousers of my youth remember my form.

Speed is the alternative to depth: remember this always in skiing and thinking. The bull moose voyages through the lack of line pursued by something on snowshoes. When he turns, it is too late to shoot; the meat will be all sweaty. Let's lie down and make angels. Fish, birds, and reptiles in particular. Higgins. What does the moon care if water derives from snow or the snow from water? Death is no cocktail — simply rising and rising tide. I'm going out and die in the snow; my lungs will drown me one flake at a time, far from the railroad that hoots ash over the drifts. It's time to be off anyway: the fly-zipper is gefritzt on my metaphysical trousers.

Because the inlets and outlets are closed off now, no fish spawn in my cells. Maximilian Higgins stands before the mirror watching an algae-green liquid filling the heretofore clear aquaria of his eyes. So much dust and ash from the railroad has entered the water — now the water full of sewage etc. closes over the track. Only the water-snakes are still with us and they're having a bad time. Evolution did not prefigure this. A last bird perches on the recalcitrant stack of a locomotive; the rest is submerged. A good drink will change things. I'll be up for it again in a minute, you'll see. Steam blooming from one container to another, there's procreation. Words are better than snakes or birds, there's an alternative. Maximilian's last maxim: There will never be enough mothers to eat this afterbirth. With that, he buries himself, fully-trousered, at the very bottom of the paragraph.

ANDREAS SCHROEDER 1946–

Andreas Schroeder (b. Hohengeggelsen, Germany) has published diverse works, including two books of poetry, *The Ozone Minotaur* (1969) and *File of Uncertainties* (1971), plus a suite of shorter stories, entitled *The Late Man* (1972). Schroeder has been nominated for the Governor General's Award in nonfiction for his journal *Shaking It Rough* (1976), which recounts his term served in prison for a minor narcotics violation. His novel, *Dustship Glory* (1984), was nominated for the Seal First Novel Award. He has also produced three documentary collections of anecdotes about acts of notorious deception: *Scams, Scandals and Skulduggery* (1996), *Cheats, Charlatans and Chicanery* (1997), and *Fakes, Frauds and Flimflammery* (1999).

"The Connection" recounts the travails of Mr. Derringer, whose name undergoes many gradual changes in spelling as he acquiesces to a series of misrecognitions over the course of a hapless journey that leads, by many *détournements*, farther and farther away from his anticipated destination. Schroeder has remarked that "the shortest distance between two truths is rarely anything as convenient as a straight line"[9] — hence, his fable provides an allegory for the kind of mistakes, blunders, and glitches, which inevitably occur during the transmission of any message through a system of valves, shunts, and relays. His fable implies that if the reader and the writer happen to make a connection, such a rendezvous occurs only by chance in a manner whose meaning often gets misread, garbled, or delayed.

"THE CONNECTION" FROM *THE LATE MAN*
BY ANDREAS SCHROEDER

1.

"**THIS** is your air ticket and this, as you see, your health certificate. Car reservations have been made for you at your destination, and of course hotel arrangements as well." The secretary speaks in a brisk, confident voice, laying various documents on the desk before one Mr. Derringer, recently-hired employee of a well-established oil company in the Northwest. Derringer murmurs his thanks, double-checks several items on his itinerary, picks up his briefcase and departs.

When the plane touches down at New York's Kennedy Airport, Derringer gathers his belongings, shrugs on his overcoat and prepares to meet the public relations man who is to fill him in on missing details. As he picks his way down the ramp stairs, a stewardess calls his name.

"Mr. Derringe!" "Mr. Derringe of Chicago!" Derringer makes himself known. "Derringer," he corrects. "Derringer, with an *r*." The stewardess glances at a piece of paper in her hand and shrugs. "A message for you Mr. Derringe," she monotones. "Please check with the Passenger Information counter on the Departures level."

Derringer frowns as he rises up the escalator to Departures. There is supposed to be a company man here. At Passenger Information a young girl searches through her files. "Mr. Derring? That's you? Yes, I have a message here that you're to fly on to Florida. A change in plans." She holds out an air ticket for him to sign. "The name's spelled wrong," Derringer notes. "My name ends in *er*."

"Oh dear, I'd better check this," the girl worries, re-thumbing through her files. "Ah here we are; Mr. Dorrengor right?" "Not quite," Derringer replies, "*er* you know; *e* as in elphinstone, *r* as in rape." The girl lays both tickets on the counter; the second is for Mexico.

"I'd suggest you better decide which refers to you Mr. Dorrengor," she says. "The plane for Mexico leaves in ten minutes, and the one for Florida in twenty-seven. We've got to reroute your luggage, you know." She sounds somehow reproachful.

Derringer feels annoyed and undecided. He has no idea whom he might phone for help; it is now Sunday and no one would be reachable anyway. He chooses Dorrengor, signs the ticket and has the tags on his suitcase changed. In a short time he is on his way to Torreon, Mexico.

2.

A stewardess in Torreon is expecting him. "Mr. Farronga?" she asks politely as he steps from the plane. "Your car is waiting for you on Level 5." "You've got the name wrong again," Dorrengor informs her, tired and irritated. "Then this doesn't apply to you?" the stewardess queries apologetically. "I'm so sorry." The flight passengers disperse, the stewardess circulating among them inquiring "Farronga?" of every man she sees. No one answers to the name. When all the passengers have departed, Dorrengor and the stewardess are left behind. "I suppose that message is for me," he decides, and has his luggage brought to Level 5.

3.

"You're Mr. Fatronca?" the rental agent asks. "Sign here, please." Farronga signs. The agent hesitates. "The signature doesn't match the name," he points out. "I can't possibly let a car go out with a discrepancy like that."

Farronga reflects. He has a choice of bogging down at this point or ploughing on, possibly saving a lot of time. "It's spelled differently in different countries, of course," he snaps at the agent. "Here; if it's so important to you, I'll spell it your way."

The agent looks relieved and checks the papers again. "You can simply leave it at the Sao Santos Airport when you arrive there, Mr. Fatronca," he offers. "We'll send a man to pick it up. The guy who rented the car for you didn't say when your flight was due to leave, but they generally depart in the afternoon there." Fatronca thanks him with a wave of his hand and enters the elevator for the carpark.

4.

The airport is relatively small, serving less than half a dozen airlines, many of them local. Fatronca checks with each ticket counter but no one recognizes his name. Eventually, hungry and frustrated, he heads for a coffee bar for breakfast. Suddenly the P.A. system pages a Mr. Garroncton, flying to Peru.

Fatronca mulls over the name; there is a possibility, he thinks. He walks to the airline counter in question and answers the page. The airline agent agrees that the name is certainly not the same, but produces a photograph he has been given to identify the expected passenger. Though the similarity with Fatronca is doubtful, there is enough resemblance for the agent to ignore the dissimilarities. He hands Garroncton his ticket and wishes him a comfortable flight.

5.

The aircraft is a rattling old DC-3, a 37 passenger capacity propellor plane with only a handful of people on board. Garroncton suddenly realizes he doesn't even know his specific destination and rings for a stewardess to ask. He is informed the aircraft is flying to Sicuani, Peru, expecting to land there in about five hours' time. Garroncton settles back in his seat and waits.

The service is poor, passengers are served only a cup of coffee and two plastic-wrapped cookies during the entire flight, and it seems to Garroncton the service has been becoming increasingly unsatisfactory since his departure from Chicago some days ago. His complaint merely produces two more plastic-wrapped cookies, however, and he gives up the fight. Nobody else seems to care in any case; most other passengers are either asleep or lazily browsing through magazines.

They land at Sicuani Airport in the thick fog of early morning, the aircraft bumping uncomfortably along the badly patched runway to a cluster of miserable little buildings on the northeast corner of the airfield. The half-dozen passengers quickly disperse and Garroncton is left standing helplessly in the middle of the building, quite at a loss as to how to proceed. A check of the two ticket offices produces nothing; no one appears to be expecting anyone by a name even faintly resembling his own. The cafeteria is closed, an old cleaning woman pushes her mop up and down the floor, the clatter of her wash-pail echoing emptily in the deserted hall.

6.

Garroncton sits on his suitcase in the middle of the floor and tries to take stock of the situation. He thinks of one possibility, then another, but every thought seems to end in the feeling that he's got to get out of here, keep moving toward where he's expected, where a company man can fill him in on the missing details. Maybe this is some sort of test of his stamina, his imagination, his inventiveness. Besides, he thinks he remembers the company man who interviewed him saying they had interests in Peruvian oil.

His reverie is interrupted by the slam of a swinging door. Garroncton looks up to see a leather-clad, heavily bearded man standing in the doorway, looking up and down the hall. He swings a pair of goggles absent-mindedly from his left wrist. There being no one else in the hall, the man approaches Garroncton.

7.

"Your name Garotta by any chance?" he asks Garroncton in broken English. Garroncton hesitates. If he admits to the discrepancy in the name he might end up stuck in this crumbling hole for days. Besides, the name isn't that far off. He nods at the bearded man. "Yeah, that's me I guess. What've you got for me?"

The man in the leather jacket shrugs. "Supposed to take you to Cocama, far as I know," he says. "That sound right to you?" Garotta tries to look informed. "Sounds like the place," he returns. "Here's my suitcase and grip."

They walk out to a peeling, oil-streaked Aztec standing like a forlorn insect on the far end of the runway. The pilot looks at the suitcase critically. "'M afraid we're gonna have to leave that here," he informs Garotta, shrugging his shoulders with a grimace. "Not enough room in this old heap for us and that thing too. Somebody else gonna have to bring it later." Garotta says nothing. The engines spit and wheeze for some seconds, then splutter into life, the little plane shaking as if it had suddenly contracted Parkinson's Disease. The pilot pulls back on the throttle.

Once airborne, they clamber shakily to 3000 feet, the aircraft dipping and slewing like an uncertain dragonfly. The pilot shouts something which Garotta fails to understand over the noise, then both concentrate on looking ahead at the eery cloud forest through which the aircraft navigates.

As they break clear of the clouds an hour later, Garotta sees a sparse sprinkling of glittering buildings far below, tucked in at the foot of the mountain range dead ahead. The pilot sets the plane about in a steep bank, plummeting down between two peaks toward the valley where Garotta now makes out the faint X pattern of the runway. Five minutes later they bounce down on the close-shorn grass of the tiny airstrip and roll the plane to a halt. There is no sign of life anywhere.

A small herd of goats stampedes from the side of the strip as Garotta jumps off the wing of the Aztec and looks around. "I'll get someone to deliver your bag eventually," the pilot shouts, not leaving his seat. "It may take a while." "Hold on!" Garotta commands, somewhat alarmed. "Where's the company man who's supposed to meet me here? The guy who's supposed to fill me in on missing details." "Company man," the pilot shouts back. "Never heard of a company man. Nobody ever meets anyone here. Not on my flights anyway." The last words are almost drowned out by the increased roar of the engines. The pilot shouts something else which Garotta can no longer hear, guns the engine and taxis down the strip. A few moments later he is only a receding speck in the vast, blue sky.

8.

Garotta sits down on the grass, almost dazed; around him, strange birds warble and chirp like bursting bubbles or electronic static. The buildings at the corner of the field are abandoned; he can't find a soul anywhere. Two days later finds him eating berries from bushes around the airstrip to keep alive, waiting for the Aztec to return.

9.

The following day a dusty, haggard-looking native creaks onto the field in a dilapidated donkey cart. "You Señor Tarotina?" he quavers, squinting at Garotta in the sun. Tarotina nods and climbs into the cart. "We are going . . ." the native explains and cracks his long, frayed whip.

CHRISTOPHER DEWDNEY 1951–

Christopher Dewdney (b. London, ON) has produced numerous books of poetry, including *A Palaeozoic Geology of London, Ontario* (1973), *Fovea Centralis* (1975), *Alter Sublime* (1980), *Concordat Proviso Ascendant* (1991), *Demon Pond* (1994), and *Signal Fires* (2000). He has also written poetic essays about the impact of science on the modern milieu, collecting these diverse musings into two books: *The Secular Grail* (1993) and *The Last Flesh* (1998). He has won first prize in the CBC Literary Competition for his poem "Elora Gorge," and he has been nominated three times for the Governor General's Award: once for *Predators of the Adoration* (1983), again for *The Immaculate Perception* (1986), and once more for *The Radiant Inventory* (1988).

"Remote Control" dramatizes the paranoid thematic concerns of such writers as William S. Burroughs and Philip K. Dick, both of whom imagine that our own experience of reality might constitute nothing more than a supernal illusion, orchestrated by a conspiracy of malevolent puppeteers. Dewdney has often suggested that language itself inhabits the mind, like an inimical organism: "[t]he poet hosts a parasite"[10] — an infection that allows the unconscious to receive distant signals from nameless, external agencies. Dewdney has even striven throughout his work to imagine a kind of surreal science, not unlike the pataphysics of Alfred Jarry, in which the poet might use reason against itself in order to subvert not only the pedantic truths of science but also the poetics of romantic genius.

"REMOTE CONTROL"
FROM *FOVEA CENTRALIS*
BY CHRISTOPHER DEWDNEY

ON FOSSILIZATION (REMEMBER; THE EMOTIONS YOU ARE FEELING MAY NOT BE YOUR OWN.)

OF every seven years we are entirely re-composed. That from which we are made, what we see out of, is completely transmuted in a transubstantiation of actuality. The replacement of reality with fiction is the same process. The rug is pulled in front of your eyes off a facsimile of itself. Remote control alien replacement of all that which you call tangible.

OUT OF CONTROL

It is a warm grey afternoon in August. You are in the country, in a deserted quarry of light grey devonian limestone in Southern Ontario. A powdery luminescence oscillates between the rock & sky. You feel sure that you could recognize these clouds (with their limestone texture) out of random cloud-photographs from all over the world.

You then lean over and pick up a flat piece of layered stone. It is a rough triangle about one foot across. Prying at the stone you find the layers come apart easily in large flat pieces. Pale grey moths are pressed between the layers of stone. Freed, they flutter up like pieces of ash caught in a dust-devil. You are splashed by the other children but move not.

FIELD INTELLIGENCE

The first function of an intelligence agent, once he gains awareness of his destined role as an agent, is to attract a specific attention. Although he does not know the attention of *what* he is attracting, nonetheless he intuitively sets up his own network. In complete secrecy he maintains a subliminal code of messages & signals aimed at triggering the attention of another agent who himself is presumably hooked into a vast system of agents that had already passed through this first stage. (At this point he will be approached by "the secret society" through dreams or unusual orderings in his day to day life. He will either recognize and choose the mysterious levels of the secret society or eventually be hired by occult-government intelligence agencies and be used in the double-agent system. The secret society permeates both systems. It is manifest most purely however in its own self-generated rituals of omniscient paranoia & symbolic self-denial in all fields of knowledge and secrecy. These pursuits are executed without definite direction as government agents know it.) He extends his own being through the invisible social tunnels sustained and maintained unconsciously by all of us. In all the shufflings of group-existence he reaches with an invisible question throughout those he meets. A remote control aimed at one person who might never come, but who would recognize the signal if exposed to it.

The secret society solicits on a personal & individual level only.

SCENARIO

We watch the remote control agent wend his way through the crowd in a store. To his eyes each face is peculiarly distressed under the warp of a burden unshakeable. Each face is a caricature of the mind of its possessor in a theatre of endless variations. Each face seems (somehow familiar to the agent yet when examined closely becomes) that of a stranger. Strangers playing a role familiar only because the workings of remote control lend a prenatural significance to their parts in a production where no detail is too insignificant, where there are no lead roles. At this the remote control agent smiles.

The face is the flowerhead of the brain, is to the soul as the cat's tail is to his mood. Each face is actually a brain thinly disguised as a face. Head accidents reveal how superficial this face is. (Yet on a clear night you can hear the crickets ring forever.)

The remote control agent remains in pure observation and proceeds into rough quadrants. Although the price of membership into remote control was complete insanity he had made the bargain. He pauses in alcoves or in behind doors in order to avoid people he knows. When they pass him he follows them at a discrete distance always a few people behind, keeping out of sight. He ascertains when his image is reflected into their visual range by oblique store windows and makes grotesque and threatening gestures knowing full well that his friend will register his image only unconsciously and never consciously. He hates to kill the sweet and beautiful agents that love him.

He is constantly writing his observations in notes on a pad in his right pocket. His hand and pen are concealed in his voluminous pocket where he has laboriously trained himself to write and turn pages without looking. These notes, greatly advantageous in revealing the nature of his own mind, must also be constructed in the language of remote control. This is very hard and demands almost impossible effort. Remote control never asked for the messages nor replied in any manner. Rather the messages were *demanded* by remote control in the sympathetic vibration of a crystal deep within the agent that intuited remote control's insistent and urgent demands. Although the remote control demands, his trial and error approach to each day, each week, leads to a secret and undeniable conviction that yes, this is what remote control wishes, what had been expected. The agent knew rather that remote control was coming closer and closer. He felt sure of its coded presence and its intangible song hummed softly at times in his brain.

FROM A HANDBOOK OF REMOTE CONTROL

1. POINT OF ENTRY

In every human mind there are areas of ignorance. With some it is mathematics, with others mechanics or linguistics or with some even science. These are the dark zones in the mind of western man. Within this zone which everyone possesses there is room for almost infinite distortion. Using this area as a starting point the remote control agent can slowly erode a particular person's concept & perception of the universe. Unthought of possibilities, suddenly hostile and chaotic, appear in the once peaceful universe of the attacked mind.

2. INDIVIDUAL TO INDIVIDUAL

The remote control personality constructs a meticulous lie around another being. Particle by particle the solid reality that composed the allegorical ground he stood on is replaced by fantasies and lies (fossilization). This work, once attained, creates a time loophole, a backwater where reality and time stand halted. The remote control agent hides in this cul de sac until he builds up enough energy to attempt a group control situation. At any point a skillful agent can reverse the process and replace fantasy with reality so smoothly the individual does not even know his feet ever left the ground.

3. GROUP CONTROL

An intrinsic part of remote control next to individual to individual modulation is the subliminal manipulation of large groups of people through the use of false personalities by the agent. The remote control personality, intuitively attuned to the desires & causal networks operative in all humans, performs the "mean" role induced by the group as a whole. This role usually absorbs any negative or dangerous outbursts of the group in a sponge of over-reaction (an archetypal energy drain that must always be shielded from the perception of the group). The agent uses his flexible personality to deceive the others into thinking, for example, that he is dull or unperceptive, allowing him to pick up information they might otherwise have deigned to mention if their defences were up. He must role with the punches.

With such a field around him he ceases to exist in the ordinary sense and is free to consciously choose & design the flow of events around him. One word spoken softly behind a person in the room speaking will fester slowly in the speaker's unconscious until it produces a physical manifestation in that person's conversation later on that evening. Many such "plants," placed properly & with enough people, lead to an absolute control of these groups.

Once the vision of an entire social grouping of humans has been distorted it is easy to use this flawless background, this torrent of water, to surround & completely isolate an individual out of *even* this context. These individuals are highly useful for their double enclosure of unreality renders them plastic in the hands of remote control. At no time in this whole process is The Continuum interrupted for any of the humans involved. Only the Agent is immaculately monitoring the piecemeal replacement of truth with lies. People who catch on, and there are few in society that do, are hopeless "paranoids" of course. The recent attainment of remote control during the second world war is equal in effect to the invention of language.

4. FIELD OVERLAPPING

A remote control agent is always on the look-out for overlapping in remote control energy territories. The usual manifestation of this overlapping (of say two groups of forty people in the hands of two separate remote control agents) is the sudden appearance of "mental illness" in say four people. These individuals caught between two conflicting remote control territories have no recourse but by schizophrenia because of dual & conflicting possessions of their behaviour. The crucial point here is which agent notices the incipient personality disorders first & is able to use that situation to force another remote control agent to disclose himself.

*Knowledge is criminal negligence.

*Knowledge is membership.

5. TRACING

The remote control agent "tags" his statements before he inserts them into the mainstream of human communication. He is always aware, in a perfect memory, of all his previous actions & utterances. He watches carefully as his statement, his RADIOACTIVE particle disappears into the mind of another person. He loses sight of it. After a while it re-surfaces in a state of strange mutation having travelled through the minds of two or even five people. This mutation & change of the original "tagged statement" allows the remote control personality to reconstruct the processes working in the minds of those individuals concerned. They are helpless in the light of this scrutiny which uses absolute degrees of "fixedness" to measure their distortion. A remote control agent might implant an ego-flattering fantasy construct of minor proportions in the mind of another he wishes to study (even at times doing this aloud in the full conscious monitoring-studio of the other person) and see it emerge from a friend of that individual a week later having been related to him as part of the original individual's personal mythology.

6. ANTIMATTER

"In order to satiate his control and the immense negative vacuum it occupies in human terms the agent must pay the exact penance required of such power by nature itself."

Rothechilde

Existing in a paradox legalized by time the agent becomes artificial in the harmonizing rain of destinies. The self-perpetuating remote control group blends softly into the brocade of humanity. The identity of the agent is revealed to those within his control zone and the System automatically *convinces* the two functions. With each soul of the controlled the agent realizes another heat-shield to cushion his re-entry. The host surrounding, entranced by their own destruction & his incorporation into the world.

THE SONG OF REMOTE CONTROL

Give yourselves up to Remote Control.
There is no choice, either you come knowing
or not knowing. You come.

Grovel like newborn in total submission
throwing away jewels & watches in
profusion to our sweet robbers.
Give up totally.
Step down from the control tower &
marvel at the jets colliding in brilliant explosions
over the airstrip. Grimace
piss with fear if you like,
then give up.
Give up like a joyful suicide
gracefully from a high building.
Give up like the never-to-be-born are giving up.
Give yourselves over to Remote Control.
We will take care of everything.

Give up.

MATT COHEN 1942-1999

Matt Cohen (b. Kingston, ON) wrote numerous books of fiction, including *Korsoniloff* (1969), *Columbus and the Fat Lady* (1972), *The Disinherited* (1974), *The Colours of War* (1977), *Flowers of Darkness* (1981), *The Spanish Doctor* (1983), *Nadine* (1986), *Emotional Arithmetic* (1990), *The Bookseller* (1993), and *Last Seen* (1996). His novel *Elizabeth and After* (1999) won the Governor General's Award, and his English adaptation of *Le Surveillant* (1982), by Gaétan Brulotte, won the John Glassco Translation Prize (1990). He garnered numerous other honours, including the Toronto Arts Award (1998) and the Harbourfront Festival Prize (1999). A memoir entitled *Typing* (2000) was published posthumously, as was a collection of stories, *Getting Lucky* (2000).

"A Literary History of Anton" lampoons the kind of *Künstlerroman* that might depict the romantic evolution of a writer who attains love in youth, betrays love for glory, and regains love at death; instead, Cohen parodies the narcissistic subjectivity of such a fixed genre through a self-conscious, self-reflexive narrative, whose structural "narcissism" interferes with our attempt to imagine a psychologically plausible character. Cohen has commented that, in Canada, writers have so far produced only a few isolated examples of such postmodernity: "[a]lthough these experiments have often been enthusiastically welcomed by critics eager to see the emergence of a 'postmodern' Canadian literature, postmodernism in Canada is more alive as a critical theory than as a group of books."[III]

"A LITERARY HISTORY OF ANTON"
BY MATT COHEN

CHAPTER 1.   ANTON IS BORN.

FROM the moment that Anton slid out of the bloody canal of his mother and into this world, he was obsessed with the most important question of his life: who will love me? he cried and shrieked like an infantile prophet. His mother clasped him to her. Even through the fog of anaesthetic and pain she could recognize this voice as part of herself. While she held him, Anton felt his eyelids pressing wetly against his cheeks. For years he woke up this way, crying for no reason. When he was too old to go to his mother, he would lie in bed and wait for the morning to dry his skin.

"At least I was born," he would say. Anton had developed a strange habit of reciting his life to himself, as if he was to be the best proof of his own existence. "At least I was born," he would say. Nothing could release him but the love of a beautiful woman.

CHAPTER 2.   IN THE AFTERNOON.

In the afternoon, Anton liked to meditate upon his mind. He was cultivating that simple and direct clarity which he knew to be the mark of true genius. His eyes learned how to brush themselves in the mirror. Sometimes he dreamed eccentrically; and strolled about the city streets, giving out his innocent and generous smile.

"Anton," his mother said. "You're too old to live at home. It's time you moved out. Your father says you have to be a man."

Anton sighed.

"Well?" his mother asked. "What are you going to do?"

Anton moved to the room above the garage. He kept his curtains closed all the time and began to cultivate newspapers. He fell asleep for a week and no one noticed. When he woke up he inspected himself in the mirror. He spread his hands apart and held them in front of his eyes.

"At least I was born," he said to himself. He dropped out of college and got a job driving a hearse. In the evenings he would go and visit with the inscrutable undertaker.

CHAPTER 3.   ANTON MEETS HIS DESTINY (PART ONE).

Without preamble, after all these years spent sleepwalking through the desert, Anton fell desperately in love. It was everything he had ever imagined: a vise clamping his insides; a symphony of pleasure; an endless trip to the bottom of the bottomless abyss. When he finally landed, there was a journalist waiting to interview him.

MC: Anton, please tell me, everyone wants to know. Is love worth it? Or is it just another game?

A: (groaning) I think my leg is broken. (He feels it carefully then staggers to his feet.) Where is she?

MC: Anton, I hate to tell you this — but she's gone.

A: Gone? (He clutches his chest and whimpers as he limps about in circles.) I hardly knew her.

MC: Alas, Anton, life is brief. (Takes out notepad and pen.) But you must remember something, all those golden, timeless moments you shared together, the taste of her lips on your tongue, her warm breath on your neck . . .

A: It began like this. How can I explain? Of those around me, no one but myself believed in love. Pure love. Redeeming love. The utter burning of selfless love. Love. True Love! I spent every day searching for the perfect woman. I didn't care who loved me, I only wanted to give. One day, when I was in a department store looking for some jewellery to give my poor lonely mother, I absent-mindedly stuffed a few pairs of socks in my coat pocket. (Sometimes, when I am driving at night, my feet begin to sweat.) As I was walking out of the store a premonition of change swept over me. At that very moment my arm was held by a small hand with an iron grip. I turned around. It was love at first sight.

CHAPTER 4.   INTERMISSION.

You'll excuse me for interrupting. As you can see, Anton is the type of man who could talk about himself forever. Once started he finds that his mouth moves with a will of its own and he babbles compulsively, without being able to remember why he began. Of course, self-expression is important. We are pleased to see that Anton is so free with words. But what is there about him that is particularly interesting? Why should we be persuaded that he is a hero of our times?

A hero is a man who is in the vanguard of his own life. He rides it with a kind of foolish resignation, charging bravely into history although it is made up of forces he can neither see nor understand. But Anton waits for his life to happen to him, like a man who has fallen asleep waiting for a bus. Poor Anton, we say, so simple and naive. What else is there to know?

CHAPTER 5.   ANTON MEETS HIS DESTINY (PART TWO).

We gazed into each other's eyes. She had grasped my soul, and I hers. We both shuddered at once; fate had crossed our lives, banging them together like two dry bones. During the entire interview with the police our faces were hot scarlet, as if we had been caught performing an obscene act behind the utensils section. Angela was her name.

She had eyes as blue as the sky at dawn. I saw my face reflected and I swam in them, like a fish in the sea.

Heat rose from our skins. Our bodies breathed together, breathed the night in and out. When we heard music, it was music played for us. When our souls joined, they swung together like the sun and the moon.

CHAPTER 6.   THE FUTURE AS HISTORY.

Looking back, we cannot judge Anton's passion. Although Anton himself is utterly insignificant, it could be that the love that he felt, the passion that briefly transformed him, was somehow universal — and that at least for a brief period Anton was redeemed. So it could be.

So it could be. But as for myself, I don't believe it. To tell the truth, I don't believe in anything about love any more. Sitting here, writing, about Anton's ridiculous urge to life, I can't help looking out the window. Soon I'll go outside and walk through the streets. The cold concrete will reach up through my shoes, sucking out the warmth of my flesh as the ground beneath turns away from the sun.

What does my life mean? I ask myself. Who cares about Anton? Maybe someone else should be commissioned to write his story. After all, there are at least some interesting moments in his life. There was an incident, for example, that happened while he was working for the undertaker — a brief drama that revealed something about the very inner depths of Anton. It happened one night, while they were up late talking.

"Pass the brandy," the undertaker said. He was sitting on his usual casket, the one he used to save money on a couch.

"Of course," Anton replied. He took a long draught from the flask and then passed it to his employer.

"You've worked here one whole year now," the undertaker said. "I want to make you an offer." The undertaker was a tall, sallow man, with a deep voice and a mask-like face.

"Yes?"

"Suppose I guarantee to you that you will meet the perfect woman of your dreams. You will fall wildly in love with each other. For two weeks everything will be exactly as you have always wished. Even better. Then you will never see her again."

Anton scratched his head. "It sounds attractive — "

"Excellent."

"But I was hoping for something better."

They sat silent for a long time. "You drive a hard bargain," the under-taker finally said. He lit a cigar and puffed at it contemplatively, as if absorbing an unexpected defeat. "You'd better be the one to set the terms."

"A house, to begin with. And more than two weeks. Make it a lifetime with children and trips to the ocean besides. And, to tell the truth, I've always wanted a sports car and a mistress."

CHAPTER 7.   THE WHOLE TRUTH.

I want to say first of all that there was no bargain, no deal, no contract or understanding — either under the table or otherwise. I admit that we had a conversation of sorts; it's only natural for people who work together to some-times pass the day this way. I admit that sometimes the future comes true, but you know that in this and every other interview to the press I've constantly stressed the need . . .

You know what I mean.

CHAPTER 8.   THE INTERVIEW CONCLUDED.

MC: Anton?

A: Yes?

MC: When they find us, we'll be dead here at the bottom of the bot-tomless abyss. Our flesh will have rotted and the birds will have carried our bones away. Only this interview will remain. Do you have any final message? Touching last words?

A: (groaning) There is something I'd like to say — just to you. Promise you won't write it down?

MC: It's getting too dark to see.

A: (hesitantly) Maybe I should have been satisfied with her. I didn't really need a mistress and a sports car. If I would have just stayed at home, everything would have been all right. What do you think?

MC: Me?

A: Yes.

MC: I think you're losing your nerve, Anton. Millions of readers have eagerly followed your adventures, and now you're saying you would have rather stayed home?

A: Yes. That's it exactly.

MC: (after a long silence) Anton, the moon is coming up. Can you see the moon?

A: (groaning) It's beautiful.

MC: I can write by the light of the moon, Anton. Now's the time to say it, to give one last message of hope.

A: I want to thank my parents . . .

MC: (reading) "In his last, dying moments, the hero of love wished to thank his parents, his wife, and his mistress. He wished them to know that although he died of a broken heart, he suffered no pain, and was looking forward to the great beyond."

MARTIN VAUGHN-JAMES 1943–

Martin Vaughn-James (b. Bristol, England) is the author of several visual novels, including *Elephant* (1970), *The Projector* (1971), *The Park* (1972), *The Cage* (1975), *Après la Bataille* (1982), and *L'Enquêteur* (1983). Vaughn-James has also published two satirical thrillers: *Night Train* (1989) and *The Tomb of Zwaab* (1991). His drawings have appeared in *Minuit*, and he has illustrated books by many diverse writers, including, Lautréamont, L-F Céline, Claude Simon, Alain Robbe-Grillet, Jacques Izoard, Louis-Philippe Hébert, Harry Blake, and Leonard Cohen. He is a founding member of the Groupe Mémoires, and he has exhibited his artwork at galleries throughout Europe. A resident of Toronto from 1968 to 1977, he currently lives in Paris and Brussels.

"The Observer" consists of illustrations depicting a battlefield, with accompanying captions that do not describe the image so much as the perceptual experience of a reader looking at the image in an album. Inspired by the *romans-collages* of Max Ernst and the *ciné-romans* of Alain Robbe-Grillet, Vaughn-James depicts the literary analogue of a *film noir*, but one that halts the action so that it seems suspended eternally in time: "I try to poise the narrative elements in such a way as to suggest that something has already happened and we are merely confronted with its residue, or something is about to occur and the objects we see combine as a sort of preparation."[12] Like a sniper scanning the horizon for camouflaged infantrymen, the reader must scan the text for such covert themes.

"THE OBSERVER"
BY MARTIN VAUGHN-JAMES

THE legs are crossed, one resting on the knee of the other, obscuring it completely. The foot juts out towards the screen. Across the lap is a book of photographs or drawings. One hand holds the back cover firmly, the thumb hidden by the endpapers, the fingers underneath the book itself. The other hand idly turns the pages, thumb and forefinger stroking up the edge of each sheet and folding it across in order to expose the next image in the sequence. This activity continues for quite some time with little variation. Perhaps the leg shifts its position once or twice, I don't remember. Perhaps it moves across so that the knee which was formerly thrust upwards is now resting directly on the other, a portion of which is now visible, and the foot, instead of pointing at the screen, now dangles much closer to the floor, restlessly describing tense little circles in the air. Occasionally the hand might cease its movement and grip the other edge of the book, remaining like this for a while. But sooner or later it continues. Perhaps. But in any event the voice swells up and the grey rectangle fills with flickering shapes and forms. The book remains where it is, a large and violent image spread across its spine.

Very dramatic. Almost completely black and white, for nearly all the tonal gradations have been lost, although there couldn't have been many to start with. The faces, for instance, are dead white, the colour of the paper, and cut by dark shadows which don't exactly delineate the features but merely indicate where they could be, black distorted shapes suggesting absent noses, lips and eyes. Actually, the nature of the image is not immediately apparent, the first, momentary impression being of a violent jumble of puzzling black forms and white spaces. What little grey there is provides a sort of muddy backdrop against which the group of soldiers stands. Most of them seem to be merely onlookers and one or two are not even facing the centre, but appear to gaze at something off to the right up on the hill. Of the dozen or so figures depicted perhaps only three or four, glimpsed between the legs or shoulders of the rest, are actually crouching down or bending over the blurred, contorted form just visible through the row of boots, coats and rifle-butts which spreads across the page.

An unfocussed hand, its fingers loosely clenched, moves up towards the eye, which closes automatically. The other stares out absently, vaguely aware of the line of broken trees outside the window. The thumb and forefinger pinch at the edge of the lid and lift it forward, searching for some minute irritation lost among the lashes. The thumb strokes the line of hairs from underneath, the finger rests, unmoving, across the eye. The motion changes and accelerates as finger and thumb rub back and forth across the lashes like the limbs of some marine animal which, oblivious of the group of men around it, blind to, or blinded by the cameras and the lamps, continues searching for the microscopic creatures on which it feeds, its strange inflated tentacles scratching from side to side until it finally relaxes, the thumb resting against the second finger, the other curling against the palm, as the hand falls down across the book.

The voice swells up, then, male, confident, a slightly theatrical, paternalistic drone, making observations about their emplacements along the ridge. A florid description follows, of the blasted line of trees and the muddy, shell-pocked hill. A bit of poetry. The picture is replaced by plans and charts and curving zig-zags cut by animated arrows, digits, codes and symbols, all vanishing as abruptly as they appear. The image is back again, evidently important enough to the narrative to warrant showing it once more. It remains. The voice, however, continues without hesitation, describing how they advanced upon the plain in fan-shaped columns or some similar formation, and how by sunset the cavalry or the musketeers or the reserves were routed and that the situation was hopeless, a disaster, a tragic defeat. A massacre, the voice seeming to trail off, its inventory of retreats, of positions held or lost, of advances, setbacks, victories and stalemates fading away, the recitation weakening, overwhelmed almost, by that picture spread across the screen.

I don't remember . . . Soldiers.

GEORGE BOWERING 1935–

George Bowering (b. Penticton, BC) is one of the founders of *Tish*, the renowned literary magazine, created in response to the work of the Black Mountain Poets. Bowering has written over forty titles, including *Sticks & Stones* (1963), *Baseball* (1967), *Geneve* (1971), *Allophanes* (1976), *Kerrisdale Elegies* (1984), *Errata* (1988), *The Moustache* (1993), and *A Magpie Life* (2001). He has twice won the Governor General's Award — once for his novel, *Burning Water* (1980), and once for his two poetry collections, *Gangs of Kosmos* (1969) and *Rocky Mountain Foot* (1969). He has taught English at several institutions, including the University of Calgary, the University of Western Ontario, and Simon Fraser University.

"The Pretty Good Canadian Novel" is an excerpt from *A Short Sad Book* (1977), a parodic *roman à clef*, whose style imitates the disjointed, repetitive statements found in *A Long Gay Book* (1927), by Gertrude Stein. Bowering recounts an allegory about Stan Bevington, the proprietor of Coach House Press, a publisher committed to printing beautiful, eccentric Canadian novels. Bowering lampoons realist fiction, in which "[o]ne writes a book & then tries to make the reader agree that he is not reading a book";[13] hence, Bowering interjects himself into the story in order to dispel this façade. His self-conscious Canadian narrative mocks self-conscious Canadian literati who long for an indigenous literature that might equal the great works of a conservative, if not stereotypical, canon.

"THE PRETTY GOOD CANADIAN NOVEL" FROM *A SHORT SAD BOOK*
BY GEORGE BOWERING

CHAPTER XLI

WELL was that the end yes & no. It was the end of the mystery & the end of the decade & the end of the Black Mountain Influence & the end of the geographical mystery of Canadian literature & it was in a way the end of Canadian literature.

Who killed Tom Thompson. I couldnt say who killed Cock Robin. You see this is not a children's novel but there is a rime already.

Well there is a rime already.

This is a serial novel.

Ask Stan.

Stan came from Edmonton. He came from Edmonton & arrived in Toronto on the bus. He was sitting there with an old ordinary Doukhobor hat on his head, a paper shopping bag between his feet, he never said a word on the bus. He wasnt much of a man for words. He was in love with books. He didnt read them. He loved them.

Isnt this a surprise, I had no idea I was going to tell you about Stan. He just arrived & this is not the 42nd parallel it is the 41st discretion.

Writing is not parallel it is serial.

Stan, well what do we know about Stan. I saw him the second time
Mr Gold got him high. He was standing against the wall behind Pierre
Berton. Pierre Berton is from further north & west than Edmonton. Stan
was standing against the wall & he didnt have a word to say.

The last time I saw Stan he was not printing words he was pressing
numbers on a small electronic box. Words are for a printer & numbers are for
a publisher.

He always smiles.

The small electronic box works in series. It is a serial box. That is how
literature works, I mean that, not seeming to put that in front of your eyes
but putting this next to your ear.

It's in speaking that ideas come to us.

The perfect type of the strong silent man is the suicide.

Am I saying that Stan is silent. No I am saying that he is not much of a man
for words.

There is a strong possibility that he will print these words.

You would be surprised how often publishers get into novels.

At Stan's place the novelists get into the publishing business. This is
not Canadian literature. It is mindless beaver freaks. The beaver is not a
national emblem it is a union label.

Ask Stan.

Ask him why he has a printing press & a beaver on his books while the
Nationalists have a foreign spider on their books & an alien owner & post-
graduate degrees from across the line.

Forgive this ranting. It is the middle of the novel, where all the axes are
ground. It is the ground work.

CHAPTER XLII

It is the ground sense necessary.

 We all grow out of the ground & that is the way we grow. I grew out of obdurate ground in the Okanagan Valley, stones & sand, & when I go back to the desert I feel called on to pronounce it beautiful.

& if you say this isnt the way a novel is supposed to grow what can I say. What the hell, am I supposed to decide what Stan did next.

 If you expect me to do that well why dont you follow me around for a day & make me be continuous. I'll put a few dishes in the dishwasher & you say a job worth doing is a job worth doing well.

Well I see Stan once in a while maybe once a year & we exchange a few words. He has never come off second in the deal.

 He has both his feet on the ground.

 None of his authors has ever drowned.

 Where he grew up there are rivers & lakes & ponds & creeks & he never once fell victim to any of them.

 A lot of water has gone over the dam since then. Take one look at him & you know the ground he grew out of. Alberta, & not southern Alberta where the ones who all look the same live. This all happened a few minutes ago. Standing in a doorway in Toronto you recognize this in an instant.

You will notice I'm not ranting about them & us now. This is a philosophical novel, where all is considered, reasoned, balanced & here goes number four again. I always used to list three & now I list four. I am in my forties & so is this book. We breathe together.

 This is the conspiratorial view of history.

 Canadian history is conspiring to write history.

When he was a baby in Alberta he knew nothing, people poked him & dandled him & cooed at him & askt them what his name was & he was a baby named Stan.

Isnt that funny. A baby named Stan.

This is a short sad book but it has funny stuff in it. A baby named Stan is as funny as the great Canadian sonnet.

Here you have a five star important message about post-modern publishing.

Even a three-year-old kid named Stan is pretty funny. Even in Alberta where a lot of things that are funny arent thought to be funny.

They would try to get the queen to wear a white cowboy hat in Alberta.

Stan came out of Alberta wearing a black Doukhobor hat.

Pretty soon all the Toronto hippies were wearing black Doukhobor hats.

Al the detective never wore a hat. He wore a twenty-year-old necktie with a five-year-old knot in it.

He thought everything Stan printed was a hoax. He thought it grew in foreign ground. He was a suspicious detective & not much of a detective.

CHAPTER XLIII

Now you dont have a novel unless you have a person & then you have a person talking to another person & later on perhaps many people but usually a person talking to another person.

Stan is running water in the bathtub, & in comes Carol wearing nothing but some beads around her waist. Why do we say Stan, because we have been talking about Stan, & that's the way it goes, the novel.

It could have been Laurier Lapierre. They were in the back of the crowd that was watching Carol having a bath & Stan began talking with Laurier Lapierre. He said you are very British Laurier because you are wearing a shirt & tie & two sweaters & a waistcoat & a jacket. Are you wearing long underwear.

Yes I am, said Laurier.

& you keep cool, dont you.

Yes I do, said Laurier. Does that really mean I am British.

Stan gestured to a person nearby, with sandy thick hair & a sweater under his jacket. See him? You're English arent you, he askt the man. Yes I am said the Englishman. So you see said Stan.

Laurier lookt proud. He tried to make an English moue.

You should get a bunch of sports car suits said Stan, & some white shoes.

Going out the door Laurier was holding a walking stick. He gestured to his shoe lifted up behind him. It was a white sandal.

That's not right thought Stan, but he was surprised.

Oh did you want to take a bath too, he said to Carol. For a man with little time for words he was talking a lot so maybe it wasnt Stan maybe it was me. I can do anything I want with people in a novel, & then the publisher can decide what to do with it.

123

On television Jack McClelland askt me when I was going to write another novel for him.

How about a short sad book I askt him.

He didnt seem to like that idea.

It was just an idea.

I cant do anything I want anyway. What I want to do is write a novel in which I will not be able to write what I want.

A ghost-ridden novel.

Stan didnt want to take a bath. He was running the water because he had taken a long happy piss in the tub & it wasnt draining well though there were two holes, one at the end & one at the middle. He had heard Carol telling Vic that she was thinking of having a bath & he thought the door was lockt & it really was me you know & the pee went on a lot longer than I expected & it wasnt all that happy for that reason it was filled with anxiety.

I'll wait for both of you said Stan, he was relieved to see that it lookt as if nothing was in the tub but some clear tap water.

On the door it said The Family of Vic D'Or. This was the peopling of the landscape, a typical pun inside the coach house.

CHAPTER XLIV

You want to write about the country you love & this is where you have to start, with one person & the other person. The whole world is that way & so is a novel. In Canada the novel is not writing the novel, two people are, all the time.

That is why Laurier Lapierre is always interviewing someone & why he is truly bicultural & why he is in the novel or on CBC. Two Solitudes was all wrong. Two solitudes may be very modern but they will not make a novel.

Laurier Lapierre was interviewing John A. Macdonald on CBC. He askt him about the National Policy.

We have to keep the CPR out of Montana & get Evangeline back from Louisiana, said Big Mac.

Now that's not bicultural.

Not even with Black Diamond Cheese.

Nibbling on Black Diamond Cheese, Stan listened to the novel on the radio. He was adding up figures that told the true story of Canadian publishing.

If they dont want to read Canadian novels, you cant stop them said one of the girls in the office. She was wearing a tee shirt with a picture of Laurier Lapierre on it. Her name was Marie-Ange.

Isnt that a Scottish name, askt Stan.

You fool, you poule, she said.

Her full flow of talk was assuming obsessive proportions, it seemed to me.

Naturally Marie-Ange, far from stupid, senst this, & putting down the Ferré disc she went out of the press room more quickly, if anything, than she'd entered. You're a cold fish, I told myself. You might have been nicer. Must be the change in the weather.

It was raining nickels again.

The huge chimney stack in Sudbury was malfunctioning, spewing currency all over Northern Ontario & as far south as Rochester, New York. There a second-genration American named Gabe Dumont pickt up a coin & turned it over.

First time I ever saw a beaver, he said aloud.

When was the first time you ever saw a beaver, Laurier was asking John. They had settled into a kind of familiarity bestowed by the soundproof studio. On radio the public could not see John's bottle of Mortlach single malt.

To tell you the truth I've never seen one, Lory, said the PM.

Well, while we're making confessions, I can tell you that I've never seen them pouring hot maple syrup on the snow, said Laurier Lapierre, cool as a cucumber in his two sweaters & jacket. Even under colour lamps on TV he never broke into a sweat.

You know, Lory, I think that maple syrup business is just in text books, or back east, said the PM.

Stan wasnt listening any more. He was following Marie-Ange's footsteps in the snow of the back alley behind Huron Street.

He didnt know why he was following her but she was as sweet as maple sugar pie & he was a publisher in pursuit of the Pretty Good Canadian Novel.

CHAPTER XLV

Am I supposed to decide what Stan did next. Is Stan supposed to decide what he did next. I insist, I still insist that this is not Canadian literature written by somebody with a Scottish name. In the U.S.A. there arent many Scottish names. In Canadian literature there are almost nothing but Scottish names. This is a northern country, that is the latest line in Canadian literature.

Stan followed her footprints thru the snow, you see the chapters develop from one to the next, & here is the snow again, I sit here coldly composing the text. Consciousness is how it is composed.

He followed her footprints all night. They were headed east. Toward the text books.

In the morning he found himself in front of David's house.

David opened his eyes. April air pluckt at the curtains like breath behind a veil. It held a hint of real warmth to come, but the linen chill of the night still sharpened it. Clean limb shadows palpitated with precision & immaculacy on the breathing ground outside. The whole morning glistened fresh as the flesh of an alder sapling when the bark was first peeled from it to make a whistle. It glinted bright as the split rock-maple, flashing for a minute in the sun as it was tost onto the woodpile.

Jesus, I feel shitty in the morning, thought David. All this description & sentimentality feels like a bloody screech hangover.

He went to the window to see what it really lookt like. There was Stan, who had just made some limited edition prints in the fresh brown snow.

What you looking for, Stan, he said, his mind fighting to put down a simile about light sparkling off a flounder newly pulled out of the morning Atlantic.

Have you seen the Pretty Good Canadian Novel, askt Stan.

Funny, they were just talking about that on the CBC, remarkt David, all the time watching the ground breathing the first breaths of a promise thru the mantle of morning whiteness.

Who was, said Stan, nearly asleep with exhaustion. I should have worn snowshoes, he thought.

A couple of guys with Scottish names, said David.

I shouldnt have found myself in front of David's house, Stan thought. He did.

The whole morning glistened like the brilliance of an RCMP flashlight on the teeth of Tom Thompson's corpse.

It did.

What were they talking about, askt Stan, trying to be polite & thinking too that any time now David would be buckling on some snowshoes & striding purposively & lonely over the carpet of new snow. He was that sort of boy.

They mentioned shooting a pig with a .22, shooting a calf with a '30-.30, following a girl thru the streets.

Oh, the great Canadian culture hunt, said Stan.

As he walkt off eastward, David shouted after him, I hope you find her. There followed a series of similies, but Stan was out of earshot.

CHAPTER XLVI

Novels always have the emotion of the novelist in them. Thick heart felt emotion. The blood of others pumpt by the man in the attic.

& people say why are you doing archaic avant-garde writing. This is warmed over Gertrude Stein there I said her name why are you doing it.

They mean I'm not allowed to do it.

If I do it it is an accident & if I do it it is right because she was looking for how the mind works & if she found out I can find out accidentally, I have a mind.

The spirit is willing.

It is a ghost-written novel but it is not the ghost of Miss Stein it is the ghost of the novel. Alive & kicking.

So I'll watch, nasty me, you kicking whores pass. Remember that's a slit thru the romantic.

Stan the man we were following was cold on the trail that spring of the Pretty Good Canadian Novel. He followed her bilingual heart down the St Lawrence River where Canadian history happened in the text books.

Spring leapt quickly into full summer that year. One day people woke & saw that the buds had become leaves & the mud dried into friable earth. There was great activity over all the parish as the planting was completed. Before it was finisht the first blackflies appeared in the spruce of the distant forest; then they were in the maple grove on the ridge behind the Tallard land. By the Queen's birthday or May twenty-fourth it was almost as hot as mid-summer. The heat simmered in delicate gossamers along the surface of the plain, cloud formations built themselves up thru the mornings, & by afternoon they were majestic above the river. The first green shoots of the seeds that had been consecrated on Saint Marc's Day appeared above the soil in the sunshine. Quebec was really being described.

Stan askt everyone he saw whether they had seen the Pretty Good Canadian Novel heading this way. Nobody could understand a word he said.

"Imaginieres frontières de la transparence," they shouted.

"Je suis un fils déchu de race surhumaine," they cried.

What, said Stan, his Alberta Doukhobor hat shading his eyes. What.

"Je n'ai pas de nom, anonyme, je suis anonyme," they snarled, waving their crude hoes & rakes as they stood in the rocky soil where the consecrated shoots made spots of green under the majestic clouds.

The clouds were brown, & composed chiefly of iron sulphide.

I've publisht Nicole Brossard, yelled Stan, I've publisht Victor-Lévy Beaulieu.

Never heard of them, they replied. Try a little further down the mighty river, at the Paris of North America.

The place was full of novelists, he thought, but half of them were Jewish, maybe he would find Marie-Ange among the other half. Or maybe she was Marie-Ange-Rachel now.

CHAPTER XLVII

The day before yesterday I'm interrupting now or it is, but then sometimes discontinuity is really an older & wiser continuity & then you will likely say maybe not out loud well look at this continuity who ever would have thought. Who ever would have thought it.

Well as I started to say the day before yesterday I finally & certainly did see a beaver. Not to mention oh really? yesterday I mused upon how people were probably saying maybe even saying out loud, to a friend or wife of the reader, that is not how you spell Tom Thomson.

Well it wasnt Tom Thomson it was Tom Thompson. Just as earlier it wasn't Van Horne it was Crump. He is a policeman in a play by Eric (bp) Nickel. That is, under the weather.

I was with my daughter & the beaver was behind two layers of fine mesh steel. It can bite your finger right off. I told her. Even if you wrap yourself in the flag like Three Fingers Brown & Ed Delahanty. Delsing gets baseball in whenever he can.

The beaver stood with his front paws on the mesh & lookt at us, he was all wet & muddy after all a beaver is an underwater animal, thus a candidate for Canadian literature.

The beaver stood with his four fingers, no Walt Disney critter he, on the mesh & lookt at us, & he moaned. I bent over to hear, I didnt know whether to believe my ears but neither do you though I have to because this novel does not always speak to me with a stentorian voice. & every time I bent over the beaver moaned. Now I didnt know about that.

What about all you people from Ontario did you know that.

I just found out about the policeman today. There you are, the day before yesterday yesterday & today. It all happened in the last minute or so. Half a cigar ago.

"*A Short Sad Book* is a fast-moving, entertaining & bawdy novel."

— Washington *Star*

Stan was nearing le Grand Maury Awl now, following the tracks of the Pretty Good Canadian Novel to the edge of a Goyish lake. He was excited by the Canadianness of it all. He heard a beaver's tail slap the surface of the still water. A loon's cry rang out. He was tempted to construct a quick Canadian documentary fiction.

Let them think I've drowned, he thought. It would serve them right. He had seen a drowned woman once at Shawbridge, & the thought of his own face bloated like that — Irwin hanging for it, the bastard, & his father maybe feeling sorry he hadnt treated him as well as Lennie — made a hot lump in. . . .

Then he remembered Marie-Rachel. That's probably exactly what she did, he thought.

That bitch.

He knew just where she was.

Under the black shadow of the Mount Royal Influence, among the discarded crutches.

CHAPTER XLVIII

Stan was in le Grand Maury All, & now you see there is no interruption. Purdon Clarke said he hated unrest & that was the trouble with the Modern & now James Dickey says he hates discontinuity & that is the trouble with the post-modern, it doesnt have any capital letters.

Stan was actually in Montreal, he had followed the trail of the PGCN all the way to Brother André's heart.

There you are, an acute & an apostrophe. When was the last time you saw them together. I told you this was a truly to use Greg Curnoé's word bicultural event. Victor-Lévy Beaulieu is my brother, Andrew.

He imagined that Marie-Rachel had a babushka on her head & was kneeling in front of Brother André's heart, wanting acutely to possess the spirit that was beating there. She had beaten Stan there by less than an hour, after wasting all that time with the flashy Jewish kid at the lake.

Since the heart had been stolen you couldnt see it anymore but if you had faith you knew it was there & if you didnt have faith what were you doing there in the first place.

She would always want to come back & visit for a day in the middle of the winter.

& now you understand, you have heard this story before. The novelist has only at the most two ideas in a lifetime & he plays out the variations before your eyes.

The smart ones here recognized Marie-Evangeline.

In the sky over the mountain a faint pink streak appeared. The rim of trees was a dark fringe against the pink light. On the mountain slopes the great homes & massive apartments were still in the grey shadow. As sunlight to the east glinted on the canal & toucht church spires & towers, the city began to stir with a faint low hum.

Hmmmmmmmmm. Hrrrrrrrr.

The really smart ones will remember that Peggy has been around since Chapter VI & now here she is & here is Jim & Jim would like her name to be McAlpine. Around the mountain. So it goes.

That was a post-modern tag.

You're it.

Stan the man waited among the discarded trusses & fought back sleep. He felt as if he was getting unerringly close to the Pretty Good you know what.

When Marie-Marion came back down the stairs she showed no surprise.

Why does your name keep changing, askt Stan, but this was not the question he had walkt three hundred & fifty miles to put to her or to the Frye school in General.

When I was born in Dundas, Ontario, she replied, they called me Castor Canadiensis. I always thought that was a dirty trick.

She disappeared before his eyes.

It was as if he had never seen her.

The edible beaver. His curiosity had turned to love, & now he had lost her again.

CHAPTER XLIX

I think it is obvious, I love this country. Once I got a grant to spend two years in England but I went to London Ontario instead. Another time I got a grant to spend a year in Austria but I went to Vancouver, British Columbia instead. That was a good thing. Those are the only two places where I ever had a house. When I got to London Ontario & when I got to Vancouver I yankt out the stakes that were holding up the peonies, this is true. I pulled up stakes & stayed. In England they believe in stakes to hold up the peonies but I dont.

That is why Stan is moving around so much. On top of the mountain he found a stake a poet had driven into the snow the previous winter. He pulled it out & threw it off the mountain. The mountain wasnt alpine & the stake was only modern. He found out where the oak seeds had been planted & dug them up.

He was not looking for poetry he was in pursuit of the Pretty Good Canadian Novel, there wasnt much time left, he would settle for the Pretty Good Canadian Novella but he wouldnt settle.

Not Stan.

He wouldnt take that lying down.

You get my point?

Try driving that into the Canadian Shield.

He had arrived on the very tick of two. She had been there twenty minutes earlier, very hot, but pale from excitement & fatigue; she had jogged — sometimes breaking into a run — for nearly half of a mile, lugging the heavy portmanteau. She had been in a state of panic at the approach of every vehicle, thinking she was pursued. Three times she had fled to the shelter of a group of wayside cedars, to hide while a wagon lumbered or a car sped by.

Forty-nine, he thought, this is longer than Autobiology or Curious.

Here it is, she gaspt, her breasts rising & falling alarmingly inside a muslin blouse.

He untied the string that was around the portmanteau. In a trice his expert hands held the manuscript.

She lookt at him anxiously as his adept eyes scanned the first few pages. He paid special attention as always to the numbers.

Her body relaxt as she saw that he wanted to continue. She lookt down & saw that her nipples made points visible in the fabric of her blouse. Looking from the side as I always used to at Sylvia M., one could have caught a glimpse of her breast between the buttons. But there was no one there to see.

Stan was happier than he'd expected to be. This book was better than Whirlpool by Diane Giguere. It was better than Knife on the Table by Jacques Godbout. It was even better than Execution by Colin McDougald.

It was a story about a detective who, after following a false lead to a mountaintop in British Columbia, confronts the slayer of Tom Thompson in London Ontario.

She felt her GWG's sticking to her. Well, what do you think, she askt.

We'll apply for a grant in the morning, he replied.

CHAPTER L

So it was a success story. Canadian literature had succeeded. But if it had succeeded was it really Canadian literature.

Lately they have been pretending that there is a succession in Canadian literature. One of them said there are two main lines in Canadian poetry & I noticed that I'm not in either. This is happening around the Great Lakes & down the St Lawrence River, the same place Canadian history happened.

Remember Stan is from Northern Alberta. He was a little child named Stan & that is funny.

To get into Canadian literature it helps to be a little child named Alec or Ian or Malcolm. Canadian literature like Canadian history is largely Scottish.

Stan had started off with books & now here he was with the Pretty Good Canadian Novel. On the four o'clock Rapido going back to Toronto. It was a mystery to him. It was as if he were under water & there werent any fish there. Just drowned poets & swimming novelists. The hulls of American novels could be seen, dark shapes on the bright surface above.

Stan counted them. He was happier with numbers than with letters.

The train went by Kingston where they were locking the doors on Canadian literature.

The train went by Belleville where a taxi cab floated by the rooftops, startling all the fish.

The train pulled into Toronto. Thomas Wolfe just had time to fill in the last page of his twelfth notebook as the businessmen pickt up their plastic bags full of suits & went out to the taxi cabs on Front Street. Take me straight to Canadian literature, they all said.

Stan walkt to the subway with the novel under his arm & a Doukhobor hat on his head. The Yonge Street stops reminding him of a serial poem.

Across the car from him he saw Robert Fulford reading the *Toronto Star*. He was reading a column by Robert Weaver. It was about a new Canadian novel by Robert Kroetsch. The subject of the novel was a Scottish-Indian artist named Robert Six Beavers.

It lookt like another great day for Canadian literature in Toronto.

Stan took the portmanteau with him to the press & unwrapt it.

He askt the hip young artistic designer to start working on a cover for the Pretty Good Etcetera.

The latter said I'm way ahead of you, Chief. He went back into the upstairs room where he had six floodlights trained upon the still-wet body of Tom Thompson. Plainly visible was a maple leaf that had become affixt to Tom's Scottish wool sweater.

I dont understand anything about all this said Stan.

I dont either I said. That's why sometimes I hanker for the continuity you observe them maintaining over there at the U. of T.

DAPHNE MARLATT 1942–

Daphne Marlatt (b. Melbourne, Australia) is one of the later editors of *Tish*. She has also been a founding editor of two other artistic journals: *Periodics* (a magazine about literary fiction) and *Tessera* (a magazine about feminist writing). Her numerous books of poetry include *Vancouver Poems* (1972), *Steveston* (1974), *What Matters* (1980), *Touch to My Tongue* (1984), and *Salvage* (1991). She has written many poeticized narratives, including *Zócalo* (1977), *How Hug a Stone* (1983), *Ana Historic* (1988), and *Taken* (1996), all of which disrupt the discursive boundaries of the conventional, biographical novel. She has also published an essay collection, entitled *Readings from the Labyrinth* (1998). She is an itinerant instructor of creative writing.

    Zócalo recounts a journey taken by the author to the Yucatan in order to see the Aztec ziggurats. Marlatt writes about this tour in a style reminiscent of two types of phenomenological writing: both the "proprioceptive verse" of Charles Olson (who pays heed to the cadence of the breath line), and the *écriture féminine* of Hélène Cixous (who pays heed to the rhythms of the female body). Marlatt has described autobiography as a kind of ghost-writing in which the self writes on behalf of many selves: "for a woman writing autobiography, history itself becomes a ghost, one that is always disappearing only to reappear on the page ahead."[14] The excerpts entitled "Night" describe nocturnal interludes that conclude each day of her vacation.

FROM *ZÓCALO*
BY DAPHNE MARLATT

1 – NIGHT (MERIDA

LOOK the moon is up, she'd said it walking home across the zócalo where it hung between some leafy trees (unnamed) glossy in lamplight where the moths or insects flit. what is it? on the old benches, the old men. she jumped. they were sitting among them, on slats that dig into your backbone, not curved quite right, or missing green, green slats & ironwork arms, still one or two of the daytime men, taxi drivers & teenagers, still smoking, still joking, chatting, poking fun, as the night wound down. & look, he'd said, the shoeshine man's still up. old man, old shoeshine man who sat, infinitely still, head hung forward hands between his knees — he's not so old, has he fallen asleep? he sleeps here, old & indifferent. all night dark things wing over his head between the leaves. are they birds or bats? or flying beetles, knocking between the masses (indian laurel?) glossy like the night they can't quite see for lights, the moon, she said, the moon is up. something fell into her lap. what is it? a seed, a seed.

are you asleep? no, just dreaming. no more dream than he is turning, sliding his arm under her neck as they fall toward each other in this impossible bed, yes impossible, i can't sleep, o the beds of mexico with their dips & drops, think of it, all the people who've slept here (the skin of his body warm in itself, apart from hers, his skin, even in the night, even under the wind of the slowly turning fan, rises against her, solid as earth) city women who come in from shopping, children who lie here napping (through open doors, lightly ajar) the tourist & his lover (o here we are), his body turns from the dip of the bed to the ridge she lies on, rising, as she is falling the moon is rising, outside double doors so thin in the wind, outside slatted doors that reach, like guards, half open, half awake, to the ceiling, fan works, slowly in the heat their two skins generate, heat of his arm around her on that bench the cool blew, & dark things fell out of the tree toward them. going home he'd said look at the moon, & it was white white in the dark. i thought of us walking, home, she said, isn't that funny? eyeing the upper portals light shines through (moon out there?) does it feel like home? (only the moon is bright & night empties the colour except where indian laurels shine, glossy & green by electric light their forms slump under, waiting for them all to go, waiting to cross the fence to the lawn where it says no walking) home? (turn on the light, yellow walls will show, spit-flecked or snot- or pencil-crossed. someone's been counting days, she'd said, las dias, someone had wanted to know how many, keeping track, & what do you do when you know? have we lost count of the sun, los dios, lost?) could you *make* it home? he persisted (home, this room? a shape they knew, even in the dark, knew how to find, though they couldn't remember the name of the street, or number, how many doors down from the corner, only by instinct knew, this doorway, in where the cars go, over the floor & past the soiled upholstery, past the desk, past piles of laundry & into, at back, their courtyard. yes there was something hidden about the way these buildings opened away from the street, flowering away, hidden away, at heart —)

but nobody knows where we are, she said. is that a condition of home? (heart in a kind of panic, no nobody really knew where they were & what if her child called out? there were roots, pulled them back through earth to people they knew, north, particularly north where the cold light of the stars sputtered & flared, that was home, where her child was & the trees of, trees she recognized grew in the rain) but isn't that why we left, he was saying, to get away from all that. was it? to escape from roots & be lost for a while, hidden in the heart of a different & dry earth. but if you were *lost* (counting crosses on the wall, catching your eye on the moon as it wanders past these foreign trees, glossy in all their leafage dropping strange lost seeds on the people below) . . .

& you, she said, eyeing the doors, do you feel at home? keeping her eye on the white track of the moon they hardly closed off, hours, counting their sound now, one (coming in) . . . two . . . what is it? three o'clock, three o'clock & all's well. isn't that what they used to call? everything continues as it was, everybody go on sleeping (no i want to be out with the moon that keeps wandering over town, looking in everyone's back room) it all goes on, he was musing, doesn't it? wherever we are. i suppose i feel as much at home here as anywhere —

but how can you say that? she thought aloud, & when she lifted herself on her elbow in the grey light there was his face, just visible, calm, the smiling line of jaw, hair black on the pillow, eyes watching her. what do you see? your eyes are black & i can't see what they say. perhaps they say nothing. lightly, lightly, he laughed up at her —

& they were back in the park, in the zócalo under the leafy trees, they were back on their bench, watching, discreetly, the solitary shoeshine man slump into sleep, into absence, into a profound indifference to them all, his blue box not even blue in the night, tucked away by his heel & utterly useless. he has no place to go, she said, he's always on that bench whenever we come by, doesn't he have any friends? o yes, others like him, except they have a place to go. do they give him anything? sometimes they share a pepsi.

as a little breeze got up, they watched him cross his arms tighter around himself, pull his jacket away from the slats of the bench, hawk a gob of spit, gaze up blankeyed, doesn't know where he is, & slump again. that's as much a place to be, he said. & she shivered, as the seed dropped like an insect into her lap.

2 — NIGHT (ISLA MUJERES

Well is it time to sleep? despite wind swirling in thru their shutters, making pools & currents in the air they are lying in, the burning of his cigarette seems close at hand, his voice comes through the dark of the room fully awake. she wonders what he has been thinking, his voice so fills space between them, resonant as a bell — but that was the church whose bell they'd heard only walking back, its levels of sound tolling toward them as they retreated through the streets, not streets, roads, not roads but channels, rapid with laughter, with conversation at open doors, small children crying or playing, parents exchanging talk in dimlit rooms she wanted to look in, but always their sidelong glances, a slight hush in the talk as they passed, prevented her. glimpses, she thought, just glimpses of what it's like, this hidden life, bodies, within body, of land this island is, in the dark enveloping sea . . .

are you awake? yes yes (surprised at her own quickness, she had been drifting again), i was just thinking (how can she put it? & now that she's asked herself, what *has* she been thinking? what has he? no use to ask, he never likes to answer, or does — nothing, he'll say, & she won't believe it. her words hang in the air in the same way & she hadn't meant to hold him off). i was thinking here we are three storeys up in a brand new hotel, our own bathroom even, & down below us there are all those streets, all those dark adobe houses all that unknown life going on . . .

feel like a tourist eh? he laughs. she resists even the label, i hate being a tourist. so do i, he says, but that's what we are, especially here. you mean in this room? no, on this island. but why? why on this island? (& even under the surprise in her question, instinctively resisting what she feels he is going to say, she hurries back, back to that original sense of it, of island (women), something about being on an island she wants to convey to him, the ease of those birds — what are they? she'd asked the waiter, gesturing — with long tails navigating the oncoming night. he'd smiled, politely, above the towel draped over his arm, las gaviotas, señora? (didn't she know!) — but they weren't, as she looked it up in the dictionary, anything like the gulls she knew, they hung in the air there, perfectly at home in all that restless space (rising like owls, who soar through the night, who escort her to that place, horizon, she escapes (the dark she had known, they return to)

because it's an island, he is saying, once you're here there's nowhere else to go, it's a setup for tourists, look at that big hotel we passed (signs on the beach "reserved for guests," "forbidden beyond this point," something like that. they were walking down the beach, they were going to walk all around the shore —) but people still live here, still fish, you just have to walk the streets to see them. yes that's part of its appeal, isn't it? that's how they hook people like us, a glimpse of native life for us to gawk at, & don't we gawk! the ultimate tourists. but how could we not be? she asks defensively. sure, that's our role. he was butting his cigarette & she could almost hear the shrug in his voice, as if the issue were closed, a wall, a wall she didn't see, what was she resisting?

in their walk they were going to walk all around the shore, they got as far as the nightclub they hadn't expected, low & white under the trees, no sound, no music coming out, no cars, except for one elegant ford parked silently by the open door. it was the trees & moon out there, wherever moon is they are, on the surface of earth, they have their dreams but moon, moon keeps wandering everyplace. & the trees remind her of the square, of the night they had sat there & he had said, look the shoeshine man's still up. is he right & the island, somehow in its streaming, makes them forget: the square, the night, one shoeshine man who continues to sit there —

when i was in san miguel i spent nine months on the public square, he is saying, every day i sat on the same bench, just sitting until i was part of it. she saw him sitting, she saw the old men & shoeshine boys, the orange vendor, each in their appointed places, each carrying on their subtle & silent conversation — but that isn't her way, she is running back to this island in the dark of the sea, to the sea running yes to a limitless horizon, nonetheless she asks (does she want to hear?) & what happened when you became part of it? (not quite believing) nothing "happened," except that i was no longer outside it. (of course, & isn't that what she — ?) & that's why you like the zócalo in mérida, but even here you know you can feel it in the wind & sea, in the way the whole island moves. but that isn't what he feels. i'm not as romantic as you, nor as young, he underlines it, the square is just about my speed (i can't drive, he said as they both stared down the road ahead that glimmered in the dusk —

    & she won't let them harden onto separate benches (we have to get out of here, she said) & in despair reaches toward him, her hand encountering his shoulder's bony firmness in the dark, persisting: are we really as different as that? you love water, he laughs shortly, i like earth, isn't that what our signs say? it's true, she had told him that, but she didn't want to play with their signs, she didn't want to play. No, i mean really? (i mean, let's go, it's getting dark — the colours of the earth, the four quarters, stretching away to an impossible horizon.) she could hear him smile, or was his breath a sigh, as he rubbed his hand thru her hair, it doesn't matter does it?

    & lying beside him, her anger ebbing away, she could imagine the dark as an element that surrounds them, something, like fish, they encounter each other in, as water washes around the island & even in this room they lie not in each other's arms but in an element their arms move through, to touch each other — even as she reaches up to kiss him as he reaches down, & their mouths meet, even as his tongue enters hers & rubs its wetness against her own, she remembers suddenly what it is, she remembers, not the wall as they turn the corner, not the white building that says "water board, water, potable" (cisterns? wells?) not the arch & gate as he walks on, but the cemetery she saw glimmering, low buildings like round heads or native houses rising out of the dark, & the words as she ran to catch up with him, do you know what's there? (his tongue is rubbing, even now, away away from her own) a village of the dead, existing there, beyond the wall.

3 — NIGHT (MERIDA

"in the middle of the town of tihoo" in a kind of ache . . . stop talking, branches, bones . . . "in the middle of" — it keeps on talking — "is the cathedral" . . . stuck in a tree, stuck between two branches, given a space too small, too small . . . "the fiery house, the mountainous house, the dark house" . . . something is dropping "in the middle of the town of tihoo" where it is dark, a skull keeps talking, keeps on dropping, spit

"climb back up to earth then"

what? wakes up, jumps up, what? sitting up. whatsa matter? mumbles. can't sleep. mmmm. turns over. deep, wherever he is, & she, stuck with the night, continues. where was i? someone said something about a town, Tihoo, town that continues, under the town of Mérida, under, cover of night, bones complain at the angle of her hips, on the ridge of the bed where the dip falls in, where he is lying, apparently at ease in sleep, in the dark of, it all continues, this jumble, bones in a tree & hell, is the square, "in the middle of," there is the cathedral —

:R U N ,

run, she wants to, fling up, break up, out of that earth, out of cramped bones & into, whatever lies out there, where open streets go, silent under the moon. but the moon itself — where would she go? no one there but the blue, shoeshine man sitting under the trees . . . hell is having to be here, thinks, suddenly seeing him, feet sunk into earth, even trussedup in the old shoes by the blue box, jittering, constant, into the dark he can hardly bear to move, his feet the only movement in a square which the dark cathedral mounts, closed, & utterly still.

hell is this constraint — she must get up, move, even to, piss, might as well. tile at least feels cool underfoot & using moonlight filtering through the high latticework door, she enters the bathroom, dense, black, but by feel or by a kind of instinct, walls are walls & solid after all, finds the toilet & sitting feels warm piss drain out of her, drain tension out of her hips, trickling into a water she only knows is there by sound, & disappear.

he is awake too, or halfawake, & the bounce of the mattress when she gets back on lifts him, silent but conscious? she can't tell, can't tell how wide awake he is, to make a like trip. burying her face in the sheet she listens to the trickle he makes behind the partition at her head, a long & apparently endless dissipation. & nuzzling her face deeper smells the sheet, it smells thin, or *is* thin, smells of cotton worn thin by people's sweat & come, the people themselves long gone — but something stays, what then? an image of faces pale in the darkening air, between sunset & moonrise a crack in the day self grows lost in — as he perhaps, lost in the act of pissing, an action self disappears within, unconscious of her listening, & turning deep within himself to that absence sleep is, he gropes his way in the dark towards her. as he negotiates the foot of the bed, she asks, how're you doing? (too bright, too wide awake) hot, he mutters, tumbling in to lie face down one arm out to the floor. she's sitting up. we're like two seeds rattling in a box. silence. the smooth expanse of his back offers itself to her hand, but she thinks not to, thinks she should get up & remake the bed, begin at the beginning, thinks to do something complete instead of sitting in this half state, half waiting, for what? there is only sleep to wait up for —

she says, the shoeshine man's probably awake too (not even any moon out, just a cramp in the neck) & then hearing the absurdity of it, a conversation at three, four in the morning? she snuggles down behind & stroking him repeats the line, halfsmiling, you can be in my dream if i can be in yours.

mmm, he's turning over onto his side in the way he likes to fall into sleep & his voice comes out low & mumble but definite, the shoeshine man's busy dreaming himself. she knows what he intends — you too, likewise — but does he know what the words imply, in that one dreamily decisive comment, you mean, we only *dream* ourselves? & she is frightened because it is there, the absence she wants to stay this side of, but how does he know? & how can it be?

the shoeshine man exists for them too. but has she ever seen his face? except in the downward plane of it, the downward cast of his forehead which doesn't even change when the others come up, the other who came up, who had a name, obviously, knew all about names & must have addressed him by his though she didn't catch it. who came walking definitively & directly across the square in shiny black shoes & white sports shirt, past the benches, through the orange peels & cigarette butts & dried leaves drifted around the one who had not moved, for hours, for days perhaps, walked straight up to him & delivered an immense tirade that was never answered, never even acknowledged — that worn body confronted perhaps by merely another phantasm of the day. what is he saying? telling him to shape up probably. & kicking his box, this citizen left in a rage while the body of the shoeshine man pulled the jacket around itself, crossed its arms & continued living.

he must be hooked on something, she'd protested, he's too out of it, he's stoned. no, he said, he doesn't have enough money for that, doesn't even care, he's just . . . in the silence she'd said it, letting himself go —

4 — NIGHT (MERIDA

It wasn't the moon — you're quiet tonight, he'd said, as they lay there — &
it wasn't the usual sense of night, she could recapture that by letting her eye
see its tall gloom, pale light from their shuttered doors, fan making a blur up
there though its sound continues an obvious clank & whirr. no, that's easy,
easy to get back to, what she's trying to recapture is her earlier thought of him
& where that put them.

i can't remember, she admits, something i under-
stood, or thought i did, about you, no, not you, where you are. it was at the
old site & then i went looking to find you & by the time i did there was
something else. you were looking at that little building with the frieze, he
says, i remember you talking about four animals above the doorway you said
were brothers changed into animals, four something, a mayan word, they
hold up the sky —

the four bacabs. something slid quietly into place, so quiet
she almost missed it. the plane of the earth where earth folds into sky, at the
four corners earth falls into, colours & trees & serpent-monsters — they
stand for disappearing points. that is the furthest she or anyone can go. except
at centre, where the central tree grows upward & down, the observatory —
stay with up, movement of star & moon, movement of sun, its faces each step
of the way — she can't stay there because she sees him, the shoeshine man
has surfaced with that thought, she sees him slumped there, under those
trees, & begins to remember . . . (i can't drive)

what do you understand? he
laughs, poking a quick finger in her ribs. no, wait, she says, it has to do with
your fascination for the shoeshine man. which one? you know, the one who
is dying. she half expects him to disagree with that summation of what he
means to them, & he does say, you mean the one who is always there? yes.
he's not *my* fascination you know (a package wrapt & tied on the driver's
seat), he's yours, you're the one who remembers him (a package in her lap).
that's true, she thinks, is it? flashing back over the times he has recurred in

their conversation, sitting between them: she thought he had brought him there, but it was her, she thought he had spotted him on the periphery, sitting on the edge of the square, but suddenly at center, under a mass of leafy dark, his right arm (she has stumbled on him) coiled about him, pulling the jacket to, fingers on the left gone numb, gone dead, & music, insipid out of electric wires, frail & faraway, a familiar version of soledad, the sun's gone dead, nine crazy moons jumping all over space — is it nine? is it number nine? (is that your number? she got out of the car to fix its turning, it is six, six — not yet, she said, not knowing there were nine steps down — he was right behind her,

or so she thought, but when she turned in the glimmering light, he had gone, & no one ahead, only this unfamiliar road — intending what? the sun will not depart, it is waiting for someone, & they mark, these silent ones, life suspended, there in its going, in the long extended entry into the dark, they walk its rim & watch, their own disappearance? or the disappearance of those who come?

she'd thought they simply marked the ground of her dream, that native family who said she'd better go — the power of the sea & the power of dwarfs, they said, are working together — now she knows who they are, how they preside over the sun's going & initiate her in her own departure, lords of the turning of light to dark who live where absence is, at the mouth —

she isn't ready, no not yet, she will cling to numbers, to any evidence of their presence to each other, she will not be tricked, she will stay where the world is & they are all together,

& turning to him, calling him back from his own fastness of solitude she asks, where are you? nowhere he says. you must be somewhere. to which there is no reply, or there is, depending on what he means by nowhere. come back, she whispers into his ear, that's no place to be. oh ho, he rolls over, his arm unfolding out of the dark to pull her in, you'll change even nowhere into some place, won't you? as he laughs at her need to

be here, laughs to make her realize the impossibility of what they nevertheless give their otherwhere up to: the laughing insistency of skin, warm to each
other, the only reply she might make, wordless, is in the weight their bodies
do press against the dark, as they, both of them, move into the closeness that
is their felt selves, present at last.

         & the wing of his hair falls across her face,
a dark odour usually pulled tight to him released, so that she enters an inner
room made of his smell, the skin of his neck, hidden inside that fall, the wet
hole of his mouth — even as her tongue rinds his, back of, inside his teeth,
arousing his insistency, she falls away, or floats — no, his body brings hers
forward, making, in its suck at nipples, in the stroke of buttocks her hand
gathers, handfuls of flesh, to reach, sip, take, become, come in her skin calls
to his, bones raised in an arc of desire, starlike, singularity to be resolved, dissolved now as he enters, *they* do, a confusion of entering of flowing out to
him, to heat, the heat of him inside is her surrounding (him) is their surrounding element, a liquid entry as they somewhere, having lost ground, roll
& ship, warmth/weight/wet, no, sinking into it, to, slip that element, yes he
is coming, yes she is flying, right. straight. through.

         o the shudderings & sift-
ings body makes, & settles, having come through again. come to here again.
(hey we're back again) only the recognition of their, in fact, presence to each
other, & the mutuality of that, the actual heaviness of his head on her breast
as, no doubt, her flesh to his face — read for a moment in the smile he gives,
she answers, before fading, before rolling over into, separate. sleep.

a little start, a little twitch, of all direction, lost, to sink back into (mothering)
night, it, lets us float (not wet but dark, mother — no stars, no calendars &
wheels, mother — a little seed, a little dark, fruit — dark, a long way down,
& there is no horizon elsewhere which the owls fly escort to, the ends of
earth, that edge where sky descends —

in the dark of the light i am above, the light is at the furthest edges, in the dark, in the not quite dark, caskets glimmer, large at the shoulder & pointed towards the feet, they are white in the dark of a silvery wood that is weathered, in triples, like leaves, so shallow scarcely graves, stones topple crooked, above, not in, dry ground, long gone, no one to say what's broken open, whose remnants of cloth torn, into the dark they've drained — at the furthest (was i looking?) is the newest, at the end of the others, more white, it glimmers, out of or in that dark. set it straight, they say, it must be aligned with the others. & i must drop down, pull — it will not — so, take hold of the nearest, pull — it rots, its rim, tears open & my hand, my arm, i, fall

into the night. fall (apart) into that flesh self creeps from. no, NOT to feel it, run, run straight through (home?) to get away from

i am running, running, it runs behind me, that horror (it will touch) get home, get home, through, the door & into, humming, house (no house i recognize) is full of relations — mother! — & the place is dark,

they come out from to meet me, twins in yellow dresses, so you've come, cousins, smiling, you've come to the party after all — they thought i wouldn't, they thought i would stay up where they haven't — just, fresh, raw with it (don't touch me) pushing by to reach her, mother, who is busy with them all who come, i see from the doorway, who stay here, the dead, she queens it over them, this is her house & i have come in error —

turning to steal away, i hear her voice move out of that cavern-kitchen to stay me, warning "I don't want to lose that one too."

so i know who it is i run from through the dark grown thicker than dark, thick with will, it pulls me, pulls at my running, toward, to get to, upward, to become, help! who can't, from this grey horizon, separate & rigid lying, lean down toward me where i come, up from the dark to be her: you must. come back. i am. into the day we live in i'm become — myself who sits up wildly awake beside him warm & heavily breathing & still sleeping on.

JOHN RIDDELL 1942–

John Riddell (b. London, ON) has produced many stunning books of visual poetry, including *Criss-Cross* (1977), *Transitions* (1980), *A/Z Does It* (1988), *E Clips E* (1989), and *How to Grow Your Own Light Bulbs* (1996). Riddell has incorporated a diverse panoply of mixed media in his writing, and his books often appear in unusual formats, including a dart board, a card stack, a pack of cigarettes, and even a roll of toilet tissue. His books usually require the reader to unbind the cover, incise the words, reglue the pages, or even ignite the paper in order to generate the intended narrative. He has lived in Toronto since 1967, driving taxicabs and working as a social worker at a halfway house. He is presently the superintendent of a highrise building.

"Pope Leo: El Elope" is a lipogram that uses only four letters (E, L, O, and P) to recount a tragedy in a manner reminiscent of Oulipo (*l'Ouvroir de Littérature Potentielle*), an avant-garde coterie renowned for writing books according to such alphabetical constraints. Just as Orwell might imagine a dystopia in which the always diminishing, highly constrained vocabulary of Newspeak has completely eliminated all political discourse, so also does Riddell depict a parodic religion, in which communal dialogue between the church and its masses can no longer articulate a meaningful philosophy, but must instead chant the words of a limited lexicon. As Darren Wershler-Henry observes, "language is [a] frame . . . & Riddell is the kid who . . . HAS to see how it works, punching a hole in the corner."[5]

"POPE LEO: EL ELOPE" FROM *CRISS-CROSS*
BY JOHN RIDDELL

POPE LEO: A TRAGEDY IN FOUR LETTERS

POPE LEO II ELOPE

FILE

POP ELO

POPE LEO

ART: IKING/EYES

159

DAVE GODFREY 1938–

Dave Godfrey (b. Winnipeg, MB) has helped to found numerous literary presses: House of Anansi Press (1966), New Press (1967), Press Porcépic (1971), and Beach Holme (1991). His publications include *Death Goes Better with Coca-Cola* (1967), *I Ching Kanada* (1976), and *Dark Must Yield* (1978). His novel, *The New Ancestors* (1970), won the Governor General's Award. He is a co-editor of *Gutenberg Two* (1979), which examines the impact of computers upon Canadian identity, and he has also served as chair of Softwords Research International, a marketer of Internet software. He has taught in Ghana for the Canadian University Service Overseas (CUSO), and in Canada for both the University of Toronto and the University of Victoria.

"CP 69" is a lyrical summary of the Hollywood movie *Rooster Cogburn*, starring John Wayne and Katherine Hepburn. Godfrey merely states the events that occur on-screen while an airline passenger watches the last half of the film. Frank Davey has suggested that Godfrey often uses "oblique" methods of writing in order to explore the impact of American cultural hegemony upon the personal, rather than the communal, experience of everyday Canadian citizens.[16] Just as a movie might retell a novel, so also does this fable retell a movie. The narrative provides a running commentary upon each cinematic situation, analyzing the ideological conventions of such a western, reading the act of reading while we perform the act of reading itself.

"CP 69" FROM *DARK MUST YIELD*
BY DAVE GODFREY

IT is uncertain how the guns were obtained. Especially the Gatling. Perhaps you came in late, or the stewardess forgot your earset, or you only switched when the game was through. But he has them. With the boy. And the woman. The boy is part Indian, so you know what period we are in. And the men are in the surrounding hills with murder on their minds, dark vengeful murder. The woman has never had to kill before. She does so now. Let us get it over with. They are, after all, pursued. Their lives are worth nothing, if the guns can be obtained. So she fires the rifle. The plane is silent. The murder keeps their minds, our minds, off the crash that will come at landing.

She fires the rifle and a burly man, unshaven, tumbles to the ground in the next frames. We all know he is not dead, but we watch on. Death is our favourite sport. We are not sure how many of the pursuers there are, but one is dead anyhow; that is satisfying. But there will have to be more killing, much more killing.

The boy is wise. The wood is dark. The boy slips away from the firing and finds the horses of the men and lets them loose. If this were reality, would he not have slit their throats instead? Or slashed their bellies open, or their hamstrings? The men are frustrated. As though the 5.10 is late again or the subway on strike or they have run out of shaving foam or of double-sharp razors. The horses plunge into the dark, scattering rocks, their flanks heaving, the sweat of fear and escape rich on their polished hides. Do you see the blood?

Now the man, the boy, and the woman have a breathing spell. Let us call the burly, dead, man, Goodman Brown. The woman rifles his pocket and takes out a watch. We remember now these same raiders swooping down on her and on her little school on the prairies, slaughtering the Indian children. She is a schoolteacher. She believes in emancipation. She is the illegitimate daughter of John Brown. But it does not matter that she has just murdered, in self-defence, her unknown step-brother, because the watch belonged to the old man who started the school. He is Roger Williams' great-great grandson and his beard is whiter than sand and yet the burly man killed him by riding him down with his horse, the children scattering like rocks. So, after pocketing the watch, she goes through the other pockets of the corpse and keeps the gold coins she finds and scatters the few papers and photographs over the corpse and into time because those who can ignore history are free to enjoy the permanent present and you can see on her face that she has no qualms now and has been emancipated into vengeance and is about to become a river Queen, if they can only find her a river. The producer scans his maps. Eager. Competent.

They do not bury the body. There are other people to tidy up. They all three get on the wagon again and ride off at full tilt. Ondaatje would have a lyric interlude here, or perhaps have the boy go mad and eat the horses' tongues, or have the woman confess her impotence-envy, but I am trying to be true to the film and to the film behind the film. I know the men are busy finding the horses in the dark wood and wiping off the blood of the Indian children and of the old man, figuring that it is this which brought them the bad luck, stopping under a waterfall for these ablutions and perhaps quoting Emerson or Adams to one another. This is not in the movie, but we see that the horses are cleaned of blood when they appear again with the nine men atop them. And how else was it removed? One of the nine is perhaps our spy, our favourite. That is always our own hope, this revenge of Benedict Arnold, this merging of Tawiscara and Ioskeha, the good brother and the dark, this pornographic movie set in Gastown, where the devil is made into a child and burns himself and the theatre into wild flowers.

But, since this burning will not happen, despite our hope, we substitute movement, hurtling towards the towards on this wagonload of guns, nitro-glycerine, and ammunition, with the horses running free — the burly, unshaven man did not, since he is not who he appears to be, shoot the lead horse in its traces as his first act — until we come to the river, the brown river. Our sins in a sack beside us. Is there a scene of bathing? Is there a scene where a child is frightened by the tame bear of a mountain man?

Is there a scene where an Indian girl shows them the magic path across the river before her brothers and fathers can destroy them? Pick one, or two, we have at least three minutes now as we pass over Crowfoot's grave or wait for Berger to defend the Inuit on CTV and the ritual always allows for varia-tion. I pick Chronos as ferryman. The pursuers are already visible as the man finally convinces Chronos that they are to be allowed on board — alone, with the guns and crates. The woman's gold coins alone did not do the trick, the boy's knife would have, but the ferryman is neutral and simply has to be over-awed a little, since he cannot be time-warped or ionized for we are not in that phase of the ritual, so he is just roughed up a little and takes the woman's gold inside to brood and sulk over and to cleanse of blood until the pursuers arrive and blast his head off to demonstrate their brutality, their attempt to domi-nate time, their defiance of all sprockets and gears and scopes.

But have we not escaped, are we not on the river? The cool flow between the rocks, the meadows where no antelope leap, no woodchucks burrow, the harbour where there is no wisdom and where all is provided, even the rope that snakes across the cliffs that now have become steep and rocky to remind us that Eden is still behind us; is not this a flowery, earthly paradise?

The fleers have not yet had to use the gun. We know that this is false. Whoever the pursuers are, they will not be kept off with only flight, with only love. With only the protection of this last Indian child, his dream, his bead-work, his chants, his sexsongs. It is the nature of the sin that the gun must be used is the mark of womanhood is the proof of childhood is the secret of manhood. But first, the spy. The quiet man producers have their duties to the bankers.

Perhaps the lean, gaunt man is the burly man's son, perhaps he is just psychotic, but the rope curls from his hand like a snake, catches, dips under the water, is made taut there. The quiet man, our favourite, chuckles with the lean man; we are inside the gang; they spin the power in their revolvers, asking permission from no god except the rattlers that live in their eyes. The fleers descend, softly, unconcerned, moving on the current like waterspiders in a Japanese garden. Despite ourselves, we are caught, awaiting blood, knowing this is the wrong side to be on but the woman is asleep, the Gatling gun hangs limply over the side, the river is touched with phosphate algae and muddy from the logging which should not yet have happened and Wane is almost asleep — dreaming of the woman's breasts on his wounds in the harbour of wisdom through which they are flowing as the raft-barge snaps against the rope. Comes to a dead halt. While the lean man peers out over the water, his dark beard spelling death and vengeance — like alternating current. He says some words of welcome and then there are three shots. As the fleers fling themselves off the raft, towards the river. Emerging, softly, after a slow-pan of the river's flow and beauty and rocky banks and phosphate scum which the cameraman must think is natural, and the body falling, arc after arc, like fireworks given a body, a shape, a form, a pair of faded jeans and a sheepskin vest. A belt of bullets and a rawhide face.

The quiet man smiles, to himself this time, reaches for his knife, cuts the rope, dips his gun in the river to cool it, winks at the boy or the man or the woman as their heads emerge from the river and they race for the raft, now descending again, freed into the flow by the spy who must now, in turn, report to the master. It is better if you turn off the sound now; this is the sacrifice; words limit its reality.

The pursuers are camped on a rocky hill, as though to demonstrate that their horses too are supernatural, require no water, no breathings, no meadows. The quiet man castigates his dead ally for not keeping his head down, for strutting, for speculating in commodities when everybody knows they're fixed. The friends of the dead, gaunt man distrust him, it is clear, and are ready to murder him, but we are far from the hundredmoot here and the leader prevents the death, the sacrifice for which we long. He takes the gun instead, sniffs it, obviously suspicious and then, as obviously, satisfied. We do not ask why the gun should *not* have been fired — at the fleers — if the fleers have indeed killed the gaunt man then why is it proof of innocence that the quiet man's gun should be cold? But this is the tension. The fear. The edge of history. Double-sharp. We know that when the king who has returned to the river comes to confront this master of the high rocks then we will have a secondary moment of fear, but this betrayal somehow remains the deeper one.

We know nothing of this quiet man except that he is in disguise, that he has no real companions, that riding with these evil ones is not his real life, that beyond theft and violence and hatred and rough-riding he owes allegiance to some unspecified good which lets him at once play this game and be above it, so that he is closer to us than is the king on the river and yet we must accept the inevitable as he turns and the leader snarls at the lean, dead man's friends to hold their guns and their tongues, and there is time for the quiet man to recoil his rope and regirth his horse before the gun appears in the leader's hand and he himself fires at the quiet man who leaps almost over the horse and rides away like a Cree buffalo hunter, hanging low on the far side of the horse and the leader does not spoil things by simply putting one into the gut of the horse, but the quiet man is wounded and far from town and we know we will not see him again because this confrontation of man and leader is not to be handled so lightly and yet so daringly. We are all too vulnerable and the task too difficult for quiet men, whatever their disguise. Gun must answer gun. The blood from the gaunt man's arm and leg wounds drips down onto the sweating flanks of the horse as he is carried back through the ferryshack frames, the dark wood, the schoolhouse on the prairie, the wild horses, the buffalo running, towards a glacier blue lake where the medicinewomen await him. Ah, if this were only true.

But in the movie in our eyes, the pursuers follow not him but the raft-barge; their definition of productivity is based on conquest not meditation, and they know they have been thwarted. They set an ambush for the raft-dwellers, where the cliffs are high and the river will become still, lying in peaceful pools beyond this white water, these white and dark mutterings over the chasm that tumble the raft-barge, tilt the gun, spill the boy into their mouth. The king is now forced to reveal his muscles and right everything with great sweeps of the oar so that the craft holds still long enough for the boy to scramble back aboard, long enough for the woman to reveal her hidden love for both of them, long enough for the first shots to come ringing down at them from the cliffs as they drift in the quiet water below. There are no medicinewomen here. Only the gun. If there is time. If they have the skill and the courage. Luckily the pursuers are bad shots, are really, at this moment, just the supermarket toughs they appear to be under their daily disguise, so that we have our first revenge for the wounding of the quiet man as the gun is swung around and begins battering the cliff in rapid-fire beauty.

If this were Africa, a cheer would go up at this point, although they too prefer to see body against body. "Hauuuu-ssaa. Hauuussaa." A rhythmic chant as the evil is defeated, a song of praise in perfect rhythm with the bullets that skip off the rocks, thrust the dark vengeful faces in behind rocks, split a body or two back against the horizon into death and oblivion. But here, of course, we are more restrained; only the continual pattern of the product lets one know that quiet and diplomatic "hauusas" are said internationally by the young, pinched out in mind-dulled patterns by the old, as we watch the second defeat take place. The producer smiles.

For now that the third is near, it will be less, less upsetting somehow. The wounds of the quiet man are licked into health by a being half-cougar, half-woman, the burly man becomes a Chinese warload for the Sung, the great-grandson heads his genes for the industrial park at Palo Alto, the river flows on in peace and the raft-dwellers have time to talk; but they never eat or make love nor go out for coffee nor organize a co-operative, so we know what period we are still in, they don't even compose the legend of their lives to date; the purpose of this art, after all, is to show us what we don't have but long for: the clear danger, the wilderness, the clean decision, the chaste life; the purpose of this art is not to have these paid actors live out their lives. The third trail is somewhat predictable.

The river widens out, slows down, becomes middle-aged, becomes more representative of the rivers we know, so that they, the fleers, become both more peaceful and more desperate. The pursuers too descend. Ride right out into the river. Arrange themselves in a line, a trap. No surrogates now, neither rope nor white water. Here they are. The raft now is its own doom — this is what happens when we follow our own genes. The fleers will be as exposed as the river itself, their death our death. Only in suicide, like terrorists, riding the gun upward into fragments of oblivion can they keep the gun from those of evil. Even the magical escape through the white water is of no avail, nor the golden watch, the sacrifice of the quiet man, the boy's trick with the horses, the gun, the gun you see was lost in the white water, too much of an artifact, too removed from the rawness. The raft drifts into an eddy just long enough for them to see the pursuers awaiting, to feel the bullets entering their flesh, the blood on their flesh, at last, after eighty-seven features, three world wars, all these adventures, nine thousand four hundred and twelve expeditions against the various savages, and three retakes. Nothing left now except raw guts and pure thinking. Quick. The moment is here.

Overboard go the precious crates, the ammunition sinks to the bottom, the nitroglycerine floats off in its wooden coffins roped together with the lariat of the lean man so that they all float in a compact but natural group, then all three into the water behind the raft, below the raft, letting a scum of desolation and defeat float around the bend to the watchers, the waiters: the teacher's hat, the boy's coat, the king's gun case.

But not his rifle. The magic non-artifact. The legal extension of his soul as he quietly rises out of the water, reborn, stealthy as a cougar, the pursuers intent on the booty, hauling in the nitro, awaiting the raft, distraught only that the river has done their killing for them. We don't breathe.

And as the pursuers explode heavenward, the woman and the boy too rise out of the river, their eyes agleam. This time they don't even have to see the bodies, the men smashed into blood-pulp, the horses with their legbones shattering through the skin, the flesh afire, no, no, this is all subsumed in smoke and geyser that rise from the river. Sweet, sweet is revenge and the easing of fear.

Everything else is tidying up. We know whose duty it is to do the tidying up. The stewardess comes for the earsets. The maid who will clean the motel room tomorrow. The firemen who will spray the crashed plane into foaming oblivion.

Even the gaunt man is content as he turns off the set and dives into his built-in pool in his house above Speedy Spas where he finally tracked down the quiet man and shot him in the arms of the medicinewoman. Gave her a shorter course in bookkeeping and made her his manager. The toughs return to the supermarket and the bodyshop. John Wane goes cruising in Victoria after the annual count of his cattle during the May calving. They now total close to a million and he is afraid that if any more arrive he will have to dismantle the set and have a new plot written.

The producer knows better however. The producer knows there is no connection between the two facts. The producer is the only one with enough sense to go out and retrieve the raft, haul it ashore, send down divers for the gun and lay it in the sun to dry. Better even than the pilots, or the ferryman, or the biologists, he knows our needs. Knows that the gun, before too long, will come in handy once again. It is never rewritten. Its plot is in the quicksilver of genebirths.

ROBERT ZEND 1929–1985

Robert Zend (b. Budapest, Hungary) was renowned for his work at CBC Radio, producing over 100 documentaries for the program *Ideas*, featuring interviews with such luminaries as A. Y. Jackson, Northrop Frye, Glenn Gould, and Marshall McLuhan. Zend published many whimsical books, including *Beyond Labels* (1972), *From Zero to One* (1973), *Arbormundi* (1982), *Daymares* (1991), and *Nicolette* (1993). He also published two unorthodox narratives that appear in the form of visual poetry: *Oab 1* (1983) and *Oab 2* (1985), both of which recount diverse stories about an entirely literary creature made from the letters O, A, and B. He collaborated with Robert Priest and Robert Sward, performing poetry with them in the literary ensemble The Three Roberts.

"Daymare" is a playful fantasy about two separated but identical men, each of whom dreams the diurnal routine of the other, so that when one falls asleep, the other must awaken, until finally one man decides to exchange his identity with the other. Stephen Cain has remarked that while the avant-garde work of Zend might at first seem like nothing more than a whimsical diversion, "Zend . . . is actually . . . challenging the reader and revealing the infinite play of . . . language."[17] Zend suggests in the story that the relationship between the two depicted men provides an allegory for his own relationship to these two characters. Just as one man must attribute his own deeds to the urgent dreams of another, so also does the author attribute his own story to the agents acting within it.

"DAYMARE" FROM *DAYMARES*
BY ROBERT ZEND

TWICE upon a time there lived two men who were born on the same day, but who never met. Still they knew about each other.

One of them lived in California, the other in England. Both of them had very detailed dreams that they remembered perfectly the following day. They both dreamt throughout the entire night, unlike other people who dream just five or six times a night, with each separate dream lasting about twenty minutes. These two men, however, did not have independent, chaotic dreams, but rather one continuous dream, night by night. The Californian always dreamt that he was an Englishman, and the Englishman invariably dreamt that he was Californian.

For a long time, they were both under the impression that they just had extremely vivid dreams, different from those that people usually dream. As the years passed, however, they started to suspect that their nocturnal experiences were more than just dreams. The moment one of them fell asleep, the other woke up, and vice versa. They had two bodies, but one soul which wandered between these bodies, thanks to the earth's diurnal rotations around the sun.

The reactions of the two men to one another were ambiguous. On one hand, they were both intensely interested in the other's life. They worried about each other and strove to make decisions during the day that would prove helpful to the other at night. On the other hand, each of them had his own separate life, with given circumstances, parents, backgrounds, friends, jobs, dwellings — and these circumstances developed independently from the other man's daytime decisions. They could not influence one another, just as one can never completely influence another person's life, or even one's own dreams. They were one person, yet also two persons. Sometimes, the Englishman was late for work in the morning: he slept in while the Californian watched the late-show. Other times, the Englishman, just when he had prepared himself to make love to his mistress, would suddenly fall asleep when the Californian's alarm-clock buzzed. After many such unpleasant interferences between them, they began to correspond, each attempting to organize the other's life so that it would not disturb his own. But the correspondence didn't last too long: after a while they both realized that they remembered the letters they wrote to themselves in their dreams, so there was no point in writing. Besides, they both had identical handwriting which neither could read, just as neither could read his own handwriting. And since both of them were poor, they could not afford to buy typewriters.

One morning, the Californian, while reading the morning paper, discovered that he had won a million dollars in the Lottery. Without a moment's hesitation, he called a taxi, drove to the airport and flew to England to finally meet his Siamese brother-in-time personally. Within a few hours, he found himself in the flat so familiar to him from his dreams. The Englishman was sleeping, of course. It took a long time for the Californian to wake him up. But, the very instant the Englishman finally awoke, the Californian fell asleep.

The Englishman was not at all surprised to see the Californian there, since he remembered that after wining a million dollars in his dream, he had suddenly decided to visit the other man who was none other than his own wake-self, and that his dream-self had fallen asleep beside him. It was really stupid of him to dream of coming here, but he had no way to control his dreams, nor the other man's actions.

This gave him an idea. His other body, the one beside him, was currently dreaming what he (the Englishman) was doing now. But, it was he who could control the Californian's dream, merely by deciding what he would do next. So, "Let's take advantage of this situation!" — he thought. Turning the other man's pockets inside out, he found his counterpart's identification papers, his cheque book, his return ticket, his photographs (of course, they looked identical), and while his other body tossed and turned in a tormented nightmare, struggling to awake, the Englishman took a pep pill to keep himself awake, hurried to the airport and flew back to California, just as if he were the other returning. On the airplane he fell asleep from exhaustion, and as he did the Californian awoke in his miserable flat in England. After only one day as a millionaire, he was now penniless and also furious with himself for his stupidity. Why did he have to come here? He should have known that to talk to his dream-character was impossible.

He began to plot his revenge, but each scheme fizzled out as difficulties presented themselves. Should he rob a bank and go to California and kill his other body? What if the other awoke somehow and his revenge turned against himself? Killing the other man would be a risky operation anyway because if there is life after death, murdering the other could result in his own suicide. But if, on the other hand, the soul is immortal, then killing his other might mean that he would no longer be able to sleep until nervous exhaustion precipitated his own premature death. Is it possible, he wondered, that by killing the other he could become a man, just like other men, with regular dreams, five or six times a night? Yes, that was possible too, but not certain. What should he do? The Englishman in California remembered the Californian's dream-thoughts in England and was also paralyzed with indecision.

Here they were, the Englishman in California and the Californian in England, one rich, one poor, each knowing everything about the other, yet neither having any power over the other's destiny. After a few days of revelling, the Englishman in California began to regret his hastily committed crime (a regret the Californian acknowledged with growing satisfaction every morning). Besides, the Englishman was still afraid of what the other might do to harm him: After all, nights are long.

Now he could afford to buy a typewriter, so he did. He typed a letter to his dream-brother, apologizing for his irresponsible act and asking him if he would agree to accept half of his (the other's) money. The Californian accepted the offer. A new friendship developed between them. Both of them married, had children, made good investments, and became wealthy. When they were fed up with their everyday routines and felt like having a holiday, they swapped identities and locations and lived each other's lives, used each other's wife, did each other's work for a while. Nobody around them noticed the change. In time, they both bought a factory and became each other's sole agents to distribute each other's products in their own countries, thus becoming multimillionaires in a short time.

Realizing that their experience was a unique one that had never before occurred to anyone on earth, they decided to write it down in the form of a short story. They both worked on it, day and night: When one stopped writing and went to bed, the other awoke and continued. They sent each other Xerox copies regularly so that both would have the full manuscript and could correct each other's mistakes. It was a beautiful co-operation between one man. Soon, they had a fascinating short story in their hands.

Of course, they did not narrate their lives in first person. Whose point of view could they have used, anyway? They did not reveal their real names, but simply referred to themselves as "the Californian" and "the Englishman." Once their short story was finished (they considered it a sketch for a longer, more detailed novel to be written at a later date), there arose the problem of authorship. To use their own names was inconvenient, owing to the fact that they were both established, respectable businessmen. To invent a fictive, unknown name would impede publication of the biography. After some vac-illation, they investigated and discovered that there lived a writer in Canada whose writings were often preoccupied with split personalities, dreams and other mystic subjects. They agreed that he could easily have written their story, had it occurred to him.

They sent the short story to a well-known literary magazine which instantly published it. The writer — his name was Robert Zend — was quite astonished when he received a huge cheque for a story he had never written. He began receiving telephone calls from friends and unknown people who congratulated him for his abundant imagination and originality. He was too vain to admit the truth. When he finally got hold of the magazine and read the story for the first time, he was quite proud to have been selected as its author. And so, all three of them lived happily ever after, never revealing their secret to the world.

DERK WYNAND 1944–

Derk Wynand (b. Bad Suderode, Germany) has published several poetic chapbooks, including *Locus* (1971), *Pointwise* (1979), *Airborne* (1994), and *Door Slowly Closing* (1995). Longer books of poetry include *Snowscapes* (1974), *Second Person* (1983), *Fetishistic* (1984), *Heat Waves* (1988), *Closer to Home* (1997), and *Dead Man's Float* (2002). Wynand has also published a suite of narrative vignettes, collected in the book *One Cook, Once Dreaming* (1980). Wynand is inspired by many European writers (including Calvino, Kafka, Krolow, and Guillevic), and he has translated several books by his most important influence: the Austrian writer, Hans Carl Artmann. A former editor of *The Malahat Review*, Wynand has taught English at the University of Victoria.

One Cook, Once Dreaming recounts a series of dreamy fables about the gradual descent of a gourmet into madness. Mark Abley has praised this work of magical realism for attaining an emotional intensity reminiscent of Kafka, but without the dour tone of bleak irony: "if this is postmodernism, it is postmodernism with charm."[18] Wynand fragments the narrative into a mosaic of events, each of which recounts a surreal episode in the life of a cook, who teaches his mystical culinary arts at an academy in a distant village, somewhere in Eastern Europe, during a time of military upheaval. The excerpts narrate an allegory in which the art of cooking provides a set of figural recipes for the act of writing itself — an act that never entirely appeases our hunger for a novel genre of poetic beauty.

FROM *ONE COOK, ONCE DREAMING*
BY DERK WYNAND

HOW he finds himself writing chapter and verse. How the page remains blank, since the dream is not over. How the pen in his head refuses to adapt itself to his fingers. How he reads over the impossible weights and proportions of imprecise ingredients he has written down and thus knows he is dreaming. Despite this, how he finds that the recipe need not be possible for the dish to exist. How he finds a real pen and real paper right at his bedside and so records everything just as it occurs to him. How he recognizes to what each of the numbers and names alludes, and how dry his palate feels as a result. How it dawns on him that someone else must be writing and dreaming. Even as he spells out all the objections to his own ideas, how he knows that neither idea nor objection stems from him alone. How more and more numbers and names occur to him and how he cannot help but copy them down. How the mere impossibility of the recipes that he dreams of does not prevent him from tasting possible sauces. How his mouth suddenly waters. How he inhales and exhales. How he senses himself being inhaled and exhaled. How his life is lived.

* * *

For at least five consecutive nights prior to the beginning of the spring session, the cook dreams dreams he cannot describe to his wife on five consecutive mornings. He dreams not a flow of images, but a stream of words whose import he can only guess; he dreams of the names of flowers with which he is not familiar: japonica and trillium, oxalis, monkshood and foxglove, the round letters growing like stalks and leaves from the vague soil of the language. He believes that these names have some bearing on his love for his wife, though he could not, if asked, elaborate on this belief. Sometimes, he dreams of the names of flowers and of animals as well: dingo and cinnamon bear, bandicoot, kangaroo and marmoset. He assumes that the flowers represent his classes, and the animals the students who attend them. Frequently, the names of the animals feed on the names of the flowers, one letter at a time. Then the animals' names become more Latinate; the names of the flowers grow vulgar. This dream he cannot put into words, although he understands it to be a dream of love and responsibility. Nerves, his wife suggests when he does try to explain it, mere butterflies in the stomach or a meal taken too late at night. He will dream of the *Painted Lady* and the *Red Admiral*, making no further connections between them. When his wife suggests that his dreams are crazy, he will dream of black widows and the praying mantis, dreams he will not mention to his wife, who will not believe him when he informs her that he has slept a completely untroubled sleep.

* * *

The watchman entrusted with the travelling art exhibition, his age exaggerated somewhat by the premature whiteness of his hair and moustache, hardly looks like a man capable of protecting the valuable paintings and prints. Doubtless, the curators of the national museum in the capital have decided that they will be safe in his care, that his age alone will serve to gain the respect of would-be vandals or thieves. If not his age, then the watchman's uniform will do it, impressing on others that the full authority of the nation stands behind him. The curators have complete confidence in him and in the fact that the citizens of the small villages through which the exhibition is travelling will continue to be law-abiding.

The village boys show the watchman the same respect he has been accorded elsewhere. In the large tent raised to house the exhibition, they stay well behind the ropes intended to keep anyone from touching the works.

They cluster around their favourite landscapes and paintings of the martyrs, but readily move on when the watchman urges them, so that others might also see. They do not interrupt him when he provides detailed accounts of the life of the particular artist or his work's history, but listen politely even when his commentary begins to grow tedious. Only when they stand before one etching, which purports to depict the heroism of the nation's soldiers, does their good behaviour flag a little.

The subject, a so-called hero, is a terribly deformed creature, a kind of wing attached to its right shoulder. Its single arm and one of its legs appear broken. The head is completely misshaped. When they see that the face bears a close resemblance to the beloved personages depicted on the nation's currency, the boys pull out their pocket-knives. They threaten to slash the etching. They spit in its direction, and it is fortunate that the pictures have been cordoned off. But the boys strain so energetically against the rope that the watchman must finally position himself between them and the etching to save it from certain damage. They would not dare raise their hands to an old man, nor would they insult his uniform. Instead, they try to reason with him, to convince him to step aside.

The picture, they say, is an insult to their intelligence and to everything that is decent. Of course, they have not enjoyed the luxury of the elaborate art courses offered in the capital's schools, but they can see for themselves that the creature here depicted has a dubious connection with art or with reality. What man looks like this? And if such a man did exist, would he not immediately leap from the nearest cliff to spare others the sight of him? And the reference to heroism in the picture's title — what else was it but a deliberate provocation? As a veteran and a grandfather, does the watchman not agree that the picture maligns the nation's young men and soldiers? Does he want his grandchildren's minds twisted by the decadence implicit in this work? Does he not think that the face — surely he has noticed the resemblance to several of the nation's leaders — is a thinly veiled expression of anarchy? Surely he, of all people, must understand that the picture should be destroyed at once, before it can influence others.

The watchman tugs on the ends of his moustache, but he stands his ground. He glances nervously at the picture. He has never cared for it particularly, nor has he ever given it much thought. He straightens up to his full height. An imposing figure despite his age, he tells the boys to fold up their knives. Yes, he tells them, he can see the reasoning behind their arguments. If he were in their place, he would behave no differently. Like them, he was raised in the country and so does not readily let himself be swayed by every idea considered fashionable in the capital. True, as a veteran of two wars, he feels angered by the perverse view of heroism the etching betrays, and he is glad to see that he is not alone in this. And yes, he admits, he has noticed that various highly regarded politicians have been caricatured in an unflattering manner, but they should not forget that the entire exhibition was viewed by the officials, including a number of high-ranking military men, long before the tour began. If they have taken no exception, why should anyone else?

The watchman's determination to hold his ground, however, is based on no aesthetic or political reasons. As a good soldier of old, he tells them, he intends to carry out his orders, in this instance, to keep the pictures in his charge from harm. Before too long, he tells the boys, they will all be in the army themselves, and then they will learn what it means to obey orders whose logic is not immediately apparent. They will quickly come to understand that their officers, intelligent and educated men, can often see things from a broad perspective which they, as mere foot soldiers, cannot hope to share in. He himself remembers carrying out several missions in the past, though doing so was distasteful, even repulsive to him. On one occasion, for example, he and his comrades were ordered to shoot all the young men in a village that had harboured the enemy. They must have been the same age, he tells the boys, as they were. What harm, he had thought, could these innocent village youths possibly do? He had hesitated for hours, had waited in vain for the countermand, but finally had joined his comrades as they dragged the young men from their houses, kicking their wailing mothers aside, striking down their grandfathers with the butts of their rifles. Surely, he had thought at the time, the rumours of the massacre they were about to perpetrate would spread to the other villages. Surely the uprising that would follow would lead the country into total chaos. But it did not turn out like that at all. As their officers had foreseen, the very opposite happened. Within weeks, the whole countryside was calm as it had never been previously. All the village councils sent couriers to the capital, with messages of allegiance. They even vowed to encourage their young men to join the army voluntarily as soon as they reached adulthood. In short, where he and his comrades, simple men that they were, had seen only blind cruelty, the officers had envisioned a nation such as theirs is today, one in which peaceful pursuits, like this very art exhibition, would be possible. Since that time, he has never questioned the judgment of his superiors. And though he is only a watchman now, no longer a soldier, he will lay down his life to defend the works in his charge — what matter that he cannot understand their merit? — and he will not hesitate to take other lives in the process.

* * *

Stripped and halved, the great carcasses of beef hang on large hooks in the frigidarium. The apprentices eye the meat greedily, their mouths watering, their stomachs grumbling audibly. It is diseased meat, the cook tells them, donated by the local farmers so that they may learn the arts of hanging meat and of butchery. Their mouths water. It is not, he tells them, fit for human consumption. Their stomachs grumble. He tells them of the effects of hanging meat for varying periods of time, of the maximum tenderness possible without rendering the meat too pungent. He reminds them to use their imaginations, since the meat they have to work with is already tainted. The fat, he tells them, may not be as white as that found on meat served in the restaurants of the international hotel chains, but they must remember that no one has yet proven that yellow fat offends anything but the eye. The hungry eyes of the apprentices betray no offence.

The cook passes up and down rows of long tables set parallel to one another, at which the apprentices are learning to divide the carcasses that have been thrown on them into various cuts. Occasionally, he stops, nods his approval as a particularly skilled boy quickly trims the excess fat, or turns away as another wipes his bloody hands on a white apron, then absent-mindedly licks his fingers. He hopes that the butchers recover soon, so that he will no longer have to teach their classes.

How thin the apprentices are, he thinks, wondering which of them will be first to challenge his statement that the beef is diseased. He hopes it will not be the youngest, an apprentice who has already established a reputation for impulsive behaviour and who, moreover, is known to spend all of his leisure time sharpening his knives and his cleavers.

* * *

The new regulations permit the butchers to trim the meat closer to the bone. Though it will mean less wastage, the cooks are concerned: the trick, they know, will be to avoid excess bone chips, no task for thick-fingered butchers.

Other tricks: to cook the whole carcass first, singe the hair on an open fire till the skin cracks, chant around the smoke pit, file teeth into points for this special occasion.

The cooks tell the butchers that the trick is to find victims and reasons to warrant their sacrifice. The greatest trick of all is to convince the victim that he is playing a part in some higher purpose, that he will make the crops grow by bringing rain, that he will ensure victory in battle and fertility in women. The trick is to convince him that he will, like the warriors who die on the battlefield or the lovers who expire in their women's arms, enter straight into paradise, to come back to earth after three years or four as a butterfly or a hummingbird. The trick is to teach him to love fuchsias before cutting him open.

The butchers, however, are taken in neither by rhetoric nor by excessive passion. Butterflies, they say, have outlived their usefulness. They make fleeting reference to weeping French poets and drunken Russian short story writers. And hummingbirds, they say . . . well, yes, hummingbirds. How pretty, how utterly delightful. But *hummingbirds*? The butchers are more concerned with regulations: three per cent closer to the bone is what is permitted, and with that alone they hope to still every hunger.

* * *

All the teachers and certain village dignitaries have gathered outside the cooking school to witness the uncrating of a machine that has proven to be a great success, so its designers repeatedly assure them, in the major capitals of Europe and the Americas. Slowly, the novice teachers, usually charged with such physical duties, pry off the boards. Too slowly: they realize that, if the machine is accepted, they, the most recently hired, will be the first to be dismissed. As the boards do fall, however, they cannot help but add their own astonished gasps to the general murmur that arises when the machine's silver parts flash in the sunlight. But as their involuntary fascination with the bright nozzles and jets and tubing fades, some of them raise their fists to their mouths and threaten to resign if the machine is adopted. Though they know that the threat is futile, they feel compelled to make it. They suggest that they may be forced to take up positions elsewhere and draw many of their students with them when they do so. Certain patrons, they add, without going so far as to name them, may well stop donating funds.

The machine, they insist, will deprive the teaching profession of its arts. If a metal contraption of silver and rubber tubing can manufacture intricate wedding cakes, white sauces, and stews, how long will it be until all the work at the school is done by machines? And when that happens, how will the apprentices acquire the necessary values that they, the teachers, have constantly tried to instil in them?

The principal, carefully noting the identities of the dissenters, urges them to remain calm. He holds out his hands, as if to prevent them from crowding too near. He smiles at the machine's designers, who seem ready to nail the boards back onto their invention. What is it to them, after all, if these backward villagers insist on remaining in the middle ages? The principle tells his staff that they have one week in which to make up their minds, and that nothing is forcing them to make a hurried decision that goes against their deeper instincts. And even should they accept the machine, he reminds them, it would be at least ten years before delivery, since, naturally, the larger schools, bakeries, and hotels in the cities will continue to have priority.

Not wishing to appear unreasonable, the teachers do calm down a little. The few that persist in muttering their reservations do so in lower voices, making frequent mention of the human values. The novice teachers say nothing, but nod their heads each time a protest is uttered. They cluster together, as far away from the machine as is possible without their actually having to leave the schoolgrounds entirely. Two of them resolve to circulate a petition. Another decides to visit the unnamed patrons, several of whom owe him favours. Still others whisper of sabotage.

In the week they have been given, the principal continues, he would propose that everyone prepare an example of his craft, each his specialty, and that the machine do likewise. The board of governors, all men whose reputation for impartiality none would dare question, will then judge the results. He suggests that, if only one of the teachers is able to produce a dish that is considered superior to the machine's, he will recommend they decline their option to purchase it.

A roar of approval goes up on the schoolgrounds, but it does not fluster the machine's designers at all, so confident are they of their invention's capabilities. Calmly, they continue making the final adjustments to the machine's valves and levers. The novice teachers appear equally calm now, for they are as sure of their own designs. Several of them, indeed, have already stepped closer to the glimmering apparatus in order to study more carefully its most vulnerable nozzles, its softest tubes, its most fragile cogwheels.

By the week's end, the long tables in the assembly hall are laden with cakes, one more impressive than the next — great circular layers balanced impossibly on smaller layers, various shades of icing in perfectly symmetrical rings upon them, as well as confectionary flowers, the originals of which could not be found in any earthly garden. There are salads and patés and puddings in the shape of birds, fishes, animals, men, all flavoured with ingredients that only their creators could identify. There are braided loaves of bread and intricate puff-pastries and concoctions of sugar spun so fine that they must be housed under glass to prevent the least draught from toppling them. It is clear that many of the cooks have submitted several entries, so desperate are they for the traditions of the school as they have known them to continue. Even the novice teachers have taken great pains with their creations, despite the certainty that their acts of sabotage will guarantee them positions at the school for decades to come.

After a long delay, the judges enter the assembly hall. Undaunted by the display of so much excellence, they proceed from cake to cake, from specialty to specialty, lingering here, lingering there, now smelling, now tasting, whenever the nature of the dish permits, now stooping to inspect some minute detail, now stepping back to gain an overall impression, always taking care not to damage the entries with their attentions. They do not finish their inspection until late in the evening, so often do they return to the tables for yet another look, another taste, another smell. They retire to a small seminar room from which all others are barred. Hours later, their muffled voices, sometimes impassioned, more often monotone, can still be heard by the teachers impatiently waiting outside. The initial tight-lipped confidence of both the novice teachers and the machine's designers slowly loosens as morning approaches. The novice teachers whisper anxiously to one another: Did they do too little damage to the nozzles in their attempts to avoid detection? Did the rubber tubing hold despite the notches they managed to cut into them? The designers become indignant. They should have limited their visits to the world's capitals, where people know how to arrive at decisions quickly. Many of those outside the seminar room settle into chairs and onto tabletops to catch some sleep while the decision is being made. Many cannot sleep.

At dawn, the panel of judges returns to the assembly hall. Their spokesman confers with the principal, who then addresses the others. He begins with words of praise for all of them. Never before, he points out, has the village witnessed so much perfection in one place. Even the work of the novice teachers, from whom one could hardly expect such mature accomplishments, has quite overwhelmed the judges. Hearing this, the novices turn paler than they were before: in the principal's flattering words and in his conciliatory tone, they recognize that they have failed. Suddenly impatient to hear the inevitable, they shout for the decision.

But the principal will not be rushed. He digresses interminably with anecdotes about the customs in neighbouring countries, where a child's perfection, its intelligence or beauty, is not mentioned for fear of offending jealous men or gods. He discusses those carpets and tapestries that always have an imperfection in the design or in its execution, because of the artisans' deep conviction that perfection is inappropriate, if not impossible, for mankind. In short, he tells them, the judges have agreed that, though many of the works they have considered are excellent, yes, even perfect, they cannot quite compare with the subtly flawed delicacy that the machine has produced, its almost invisible striations, its less than true spheres and ovals. It appears that the designers, obviously much-travelled and highly gifted men, have taken great care to impart their invention with what they consider the necessary human element. And let no one, he reminds the teachers, discount the pedagogical advantages of a process that is ever so slightly flawed.

* * *

"Structure," she says. "Doesn't everything have it?"

"I suppose so," he says, "but some things less obviously than others. In some, it remains hidden, if not entirely nonexistent."

"Like what?" she says.

"Dough," he says, "before it is placed into bread forms, left to follow the stresses and strains of its own arbitrary mass. A dough, let's say, for which there is no single recipe or, if there is one, a recipe that is followed by estimation."

"As opposed to what?" she says.

"Wedding cakes," he says, "the traditional ones."

"Ah, weddings," she says.

"Yes," he says, "the layers graduated according to a fixed method, not unlike certain pyramids, each gradation visible to the observer."

"A structure meant to be recognized. Not a fault, then," she says, "caused by the passage of time, by wind erosion, or by the builders who remove the surface stones to raise their own houses?"

"No, predetermined," he says. "A structure that takes its own ruins into account."

"Wedding cakes?" she says.

"No, pyramids."

"Or marriage, perhaps?" she says.

"Perhaps," he says, "but only for others."

* * *

They pester him for recipes he refuses to give. Instead, he urges them to make use of their still unbridled imaginations. They pester him for the secrets of discovering, in forest and field, the edible bark of exotic trees and shrubs, champignons and tubers, or, at the river's bank, the fishheads left by the birds and the bears. They plead with him to share his knowledge of preparing these finds. He tries to convince them that he has no secrets they do not already know, but they remain unconvinced. He urges them to spend their free Sundays in the woods, near the lakes and rivers, where they will learn in time, but they are impatient. They are hungry. Holding out their meagre arms, they point with thin fingers at their stomachs, already swollen a little from the gases of starvation. They complain bitterly when he attempts to tell them that only long experience and diligent observation will satisfy their present craving. The older apprentices try to shout him down with profanities; the younger or more timid simply stare at him with a mixture of disappointment and hatred. Soon, all are stamping their feet and slamming their books on the desks in a loud rhythm that increases, then fades as if on signal. The cook uses the lull to tell them about his own schooldays, for he knows how curious apprentices can be about their masters. But their eyes fill with suspicion, then with hatred, then with contempt, for they can see he is a fat cook with an excellent position at the cooking school. His keys will unlock cupboards that must apparently remain forever closed to them. He suspects them of weighing the advantages of cannibalism and wishes he had spent fewer lectures discussing that savage practice. To send them away not entirely discouraged, he promises them that, in a week's time, he will show them how to extract salt from the waters of the ocean.

* * *

"The visting poet's just kissed me on the ear," the cook's wife tells her husband.

"Don't let it go to your head," he tells her, aware of the dangerous thoughts to which a barbed poet's actions can give rise, thoughts she would do better to reserve for her most intimate journal. But then he considers that little harm can be done by a whiskered kiss on the ear, more elusive than a clandestine word uprooted from a poet's world, a trope high on the pyramid of language, in such a rarefied air that not even a worm could survive there, not even the millipede his wife shuns because it rolls itself into a noxious ball when threatened, because its reproductive organs are located in front. Yes, he understands well these fears of his wife's, for she has no lock to protect the intimacy of her journal. Not everything makes him jealous.

"He wants me to sit still for him," she says, not thinking about pyramids or millipedes. "He wants to capture my essence in approximate dactyls."

"Poets have always had ideas," the cook tells her, remembering his own adolescence. He balls his hand into a fist to remain in control, nibbles on the nape of her neck in such an artful way that she whispers, for his ears alone: "Let's go home just as quickly as our four legs can take us."

* * *

What should have passed for an angel's wing now appears to flap uselessly at the right side, like the flipper of a trained seal calling for herring, a feather-less stump that could not support even an angel's weight. The cook erases what his pencil, if not his memory, has failed to capture precisely. He did not intend to suggest a wing or a deformed limb so much as an arm given over to weightlessness, not an angel so much as a man, an anchorite, perhaps, his life dedicated to insubstantial, if not lightweight, matters. The etching he saw years ago in the capital serves as his model, as do some of the hermits and recluses who have recently abandoned the desert in favour of the woods surrounding the village. His rich memory is not at fault for his pencil's failures. In fact, he considers his memory almost perfect, unreliable only to the extent that his senses are unreliable, providing him with perceptions that cannot be altogether trusted. How, too, should his memory reconcile the separate models that an entirely different part of his mind wants yoked?

He begins again, breaks the points of several newly sharpened pencils, his hand more accustomed to kneading dough than to applying gentler pressures. Sharpening the pencils once more, he studies the rest of the drawing: the angel or hermit's left arm rests in a sling; obeying the sling's imperative, it rises in a gesture of forced benediction, seeming to deny that it has been crippled by too many vain attempts at flight, or by other hermits in the desert, frenzied at last by the too constant sun, driven to extreme measures by this creature's impossible asceticism, his depriving himself of water for longer periods than they could hope to do, his superhuman adherence to silence, his obvious contentment with the burning sand. The exaggerated neck muscles reinforce the overall impression that this grounded angel has persisted in his efforts to overcome gravity, that he has kept his face turned toward the sun despite the pull of the sand. It is an ambiguity the cook has striven for, though he knows that others, should he allow them to see the drawing, would question his skill with a pencil. Nor would they be entirely wrong to do so: dark spots mar the smooth lines of the neck and the body, unwilled perforations in the heavy paper. A wooden or leather splint seems to indicate that the left leg has, like the arm, been broken during the angel's struggle with the air or the hermit's efforts to defend himself against his less enlightened fellows. A dark shoot, a few grey leaves and berries on it, grows from the heel. So it is wooden. Or the sluggish foot merely crushes what, like it, strains upward. The smudged ground on which he stands resembles clay — an unconscious acknowledgement to the creator of the etching that hangs in the state museum — clover on it. The cook cannot remember whether the etching had clover; he thinks it did not, but wants it in this imitation. No clover grows in the local woods.

He abandons his efforts to depict the wing, now concentrating all his skills on the subject's eyes, nose, ears. His lack of success does not frustrate him; rather, he consoles himself with the fact that the very organs which constantly play tricks on his memory should prove to be what will convince him to destroy this drawing, as he has destroyed all his previous failures. Shut up in his room, he may yet learn what his subject must long have understood: that the visions and the sounds and the smells can only be distractions from the stillness his mind yearns for. Would not the hermit echo the artist who says, "Shut one eye and keep your head still"? He will sit quietly within his four walls, will keep his head still, will let the walls teach him whatever can be taught. He holds the match to the bottom of the paper until it smoulders, curls into itself, and bursts into flames. The less than perfect creature, imperfectly drawn, becomes smoke, becomes ash, and rises at last into the air.

* * *

As the sound of artillery gives way to that of rifle fire, the cook begins to apply the base layer of icing. Even when stray bullets shatter the panes of his kitchen window, he does not interrupt his work. Any second now, he knows, they will be here: simple but battle-hardened peasant boys. Futile now to lie flat under the heavy oak table, to join his wife in the cellar where he has sent her to find shelter. With an ordinary kitchen knife, he smooths the white layer.

By the time the soldiers burst into the room, he has already applied the green borders. He has changed the tip of the pastry bag and is carefully forming what will prove to be the petals of a large rose, a red rose, the cook has decided, for this is no time for subtleties that may be misunderstood. He picks up the bag of red icing and attaches the metal head. Slowly, he performs the delicate work. The soldiers, despite their obvious hunger — why else would they be entering private houses? — make no move toward him. Perhaps it is because they are simple young men who know only coarse bread and milk still warm in the pail. Or it is that they have never before seen an artist at work. They watch the icing issue from the bag the cook squeezes with perfectly steady fingers. Spellbound, they lower their rifles and draw closer, though not so close that they interfere with the cook's work.

Outside, the shooting continues. The sound of hand to hand combat yields now and again to that of doors being kicked in and then the crying of children. The women, their mothers, try to comfort them by singing the familiar songs. In his kitchen, the cook hears nothing, or pretends not to. He does not hurry, refusing to be distracted from his initial design, for he knows that only his own mastery will save him now.

* * *

The walls and the ceiling are white, the windows: white. He loses himself in their whiteness and thinks, the walls and the ceiling are white, and white the windows, not a fleck on them, as is expected in the best kitchens of the best hotels. Men in white, and white women, now wheel him down white halls, past the white doors and doors, white doors without a fleck on them. Good, he thinks, the doors are also white. The masks and smocks of these men and women are white. White shoes. He loses himself in their whiteness. Good, he thinks, nothing will mar the whiteness and what is being prepared here. They wheel him down the white halls, past the white doors and the doors, white and not a fleck on them. He thinks: good.

When they have placed him on the white table, they drape a white sheet over his skin, the bright light shining down on his body. The white drug they have long since given him begins to take effect, rendering their voices distant and white. He loses himself in their voices. Count, the white voices tell him, and he counts, ten white, nine white, and does not find himself in the numbers. Good, he thinks, the room is clean and white. And good is the mask they place over his mouth, the only black object in the general white-ness: it allows him to take his bearings. It is a focus he concentrates on, black on white, and he receives it gladly, thinking: good, I wonder what is being prepared here?

* * *

In the very place where they have done what they did before they do again what they have done before, they do what they did differently this time in the same place they have done what they did before for what they did before they did badly, this time they do in another way what they have done before so that should what they are doing this time be done badly as before what they do by the time they are done will be different if not good for they want to do differently what they have done before in this very place and what they do is different this time from what they did before what they have ever done before as you can well imagine, what they do is different in every aspect in the first aspect in the second aspect in the third aspect, every aspect of their doing what they do this time is different from every aspect of their doing what they have done before except for the place which is the same so that when they have done what they are doing this time they will be able to say in all honesty that what they did this time was different from what they did all the times before, even if they have not improved on what they did before they have achieved a certain degree of variety and you cannot ask much more of a dream than that can you?

GAIL SCOTT

Gail Scott (b. Ottawa, ON) is a founding editor of three artistic journals: *Spirale* (a journal of cultural criticism), *Tessera* (a journal of feminist criticism), and *Narrativity* (an online magazine of experimental prose). Her publications include *Spare Parts* (1982) and *My Paris* (1999), and she has been nominated twice for the QSPELL Hugh MacLennan Award: once for *Heroine* (1987) and once for *Main Brides* (1993). She has authored a polemical treatise entitled *Spaces Like Stairs* (1989), and she has collaborated with diverse Québecois writers on an essay anthology, entitled *la théorie, un dimanche* (1988). She has also translated the work of Lise Tremblay, France Théorct, and Michael Delisle. A former journalist, she has taught writing at Concordia University in Montreal.

"Petty Thievery" recounts the story of a mother who resorts to shoplifting after losing her welfare stipend; however, she cannot steal anything useful for her child, except the peignoirs and cosmetics that enforce patriarchal stereotypes of femininity. Scott has argued that, for a woman, "emphasis on listening, on writing what she *hears*, may require plot to take a second seat to voice;"[19] consequently, Scott tells a story using disparate sentences that do not cohere semantically so much as rhythmically. Her use of rhyme and metre displaces the expository, syllogistic logic that often characterizes the masculine protocols of prose. The story provides an allegory for a woman who, in trying to express herself, must nevertheless steal words from a language that is not entirely her own.

"PETTY THIEVERY" FROM *SPARE PARTS*
BY GAIL SCOTT

WE left Woolworth's. It was in a converted curling rink. A wagon wheel turned in the dust. In the April field a fist was clutched (from the last feminist demo). "Hey Mom," she cried. "We didn't have to pay. I hid it in my hat." "Shh," I said, looking around quickly. She dumped her booty on the snow. Bobby-pins. Worth $1.33. Only $84.50 to go. We climbed into the car, careful to keep our feet up on the side so they wouldn't get wet from the hole in the floor. And headed toward town.

The crooked Castor overflowed in a browny line. Ice bursting its banks wider open'd all the time. Used to be as blue as the dust in heaven. I'd walk along it in my scarlet velvet suit. (Such a sweet smile, they'd say.) Now the frozen trees are crackling in the heat. And the city's moved down Highway 66. The river runs so thick. Heavy leather almost. Sinks in your stomach when you take a drink. Makes it hard to rise up in the morning. And once you're up, it's hard to go down.

Oh, Crooked shanks. Against the horizon. And a small red spot

The unemployment cheque had slipped out accidentally, into the stream. And floated off between the banks of ice. I guess I was concentrating on the car. Its motor/was making such a melodic sound. Shimmering and shaking. When suddenly the rad spurted onto the ground. I leaned over the stream to get some water. Which wasn't easy. Because of the ice. I shivered. It grew dark. I looked up. The branches were covered with damaged birds. Then I saw the cheque was running down the river. "Jesus," I said. "$85.83. How'm I going to make up that money?" Then I remembered the razorblade trick.

Out of the dust. The small red spot

The cheque sank in the grime. The kid and I boiled along leaving a white line. The motor idled faster and faster. The old Continuation School stood on the other side, its windows now all boarded up and vined. In front of it hung a hornets' nest. So natural. We used to sit there necking in the window seat while the hornets buzzed madly in the heat. Or fooling around. Wrestling but he got me with his football cleat. (Accidentally.) Right in the C. Keep smiling, otherwise you'll cry. It was then that the girl with the green eyes came up to me and said: "Never mind, after school I'll show you the razorblade trick." Her pink lips were laughing in my small ear, twinkling like minnows in a pond.

　　To change the subject I said to the kid: "A steak would be nice," pulling her over close beside me on the seat. I wanted to get some razorblades, too. We decided to go to Steinberg's. A wind blew up. The old trees were grinding like sheet metal.

The red spot. Vanishing. As in the drôlerie of a vacuum

The motel sign stands on the corner. It's a fish in the wind. Beside it is a steak counter. They open it up in the spring. But a row of blue security men were standing in front of it. So all we managed to sneak was a can of Draino. Large economo size. I slipped it in her schoolbag. $2.79. Only $81.71 to go. Not that I need the stuff. You pee in it when you're pregnant. Keep a safe distance, though. You get brown for a girl. Green for a boy. (If any of the little particles fly up and penetrate flush with water for five minutes.) No wonder it never works. Should be B. for a B. and G. for a G. The meaning in metaphor. I know a woman who peed G. and got a B. who pared down his P. to get back to G. The fish on the wind-sign glistened like the girl with the green eyes.

Hotel closed, said the sign. The swelling red spot

"Come on closer," I said to the kid. We drove by a girl sitting on a verandah. She was watching something coming out of the dust. When it looked like it wouldn't stop she stood up in her shorts and went out to wave it down. On the white line. Arms wide open'd. The driver smelled sticky sweet. He had hard hard hands, shiny black hair and a whisky bottle down between his feet. Elvis. His car looked exactly like that old Roxy-red Capri. We used to drive it out along the stream. Rhonda Ford would sit and wait on all the stones and all the dirt. (She loved him too.) With her bare C. underneath her skirt. Putting on lipstick. She loved lipstick. She stole me some for my birthday. "Smile babe," she said, shoving it at me. "You're so pretty if you keep smiling." I was bursting with happiness as I put my mouth to the bottle. He revved up the motor. A wasp buzzed in my ear. The sound reverberated down the street.

The kid and I took a sharp left and drove by the daffodils. (In the April field.)

An orteil in the soup

You could see the swelling river slipping between the corrugated ice banks. The boys were leaned against the restaurant windows. (Glen Miller, Gourmet, said the sign.) Watching the houses heave up in a tumbled line. Walls wrench'd wider apart all the time. By the burgeoning iceblocks. "Fuck!"said one. The cold air moved closer. The old red Capri sped by the short shorts (despite the bulge in the stomach). The kid snuggled up on the car seat. Her feet were wet. Keep moving. We cut through the heavenly blue dusk. My nostrils smarted for something warm and velvety. Like the small scented Ps in the centrefold of flowers. We decided to take refuge up the ramp behind the Bargain Basement.

'Twas the snake woman that scared us. She was in this ad for a strip show. Flashing on the glass wall. Her black leather suit didn't save her from the whip. Kept coming back when someone flicked the switch. And hitting her in the face. Suddenly the kid sprang out and ran. She's all I've got so I ran after her. She disappeared around the Rond Point. I couldn't get down the ramp. Two dykes reached out a hand. "Pretend we're three," I whispered (sneaking a look over my shoulder at the snake woman). "Then we'll be free." I don't know why I said that. It was a stupid thing to say. I saw the kid crying on the other side of the street.

Wine on the windows

I was pretty petrified to try the razorblade trick. She made it sound so simple. You stick the blade deep in your mitt. Leaving only the little purple point free. Then you go down to the Bargain Basement. Best because they don't have those computerized tags that click as you sneak things into your bag. The stuff's too cheap. So when nobody's looking you just slice off the nice unprogrammed label and stick the spoils under your sweater. Or someplace. Scott- free. What a trip. Except nobody said what to do with the ticket. Just leave it there? Telltale traces. Dirty notes under the raspberry bushes. When the snow melts. I don't know nothin' about them. Honest Mom. Then she didn't know if she should say what was inside. Uh Did those boys ever? Keep smiling. Nice girls always smile. We walk the line our arms wide open all the time.

So you can't see

Arm 'n arm the kid and I strolled into the Bargain Basement. I had the blade deep in my mitt. Which was green. For the girl with green eyes. (She used to give those looks.) We went by a shattered glass terrasse. To Bathurst's B.B., said the sign. People sat shivering (for it was like November). The basement was done all up in an Easter extravaganza. For the Springtime / Au Printemps Bonanza. Softest nosegays of nylon nighties and pastel panties. The kid went wild. Up and down the aisle. Caressing the nylons. Burying her nose in the negligées. I readied my razorblade. Looked over my shoulder. Strange. No-one in sight. I got scared. "Let's get outta here." I said. Then we saw it. Realer than real. Layer upon layer of sublime silken petals. Ever more scarlately towards the centrefolds. Luminations of swollen lumps out of which peeped the tiny little points of sparkling Ps. Spreading strange perfume. Lording it over the place like the crown jewels. (Must have been some new sort of technology.) The sun shining on it like a halo. "Oh Mommy," said the kid. "Let's go," I said.

Speak to the busboy

If only the spring would come. Everything's got all swollen up. Points in the embonpoint. The kid and I snuggled up tight. Very very easy to be true (since that old Capri cruised off) in the empty night. We fell asleep. The unemployment cheque was running down the river. (I almost forgot.) No credit said the corner grocer piling his cans high on the counter. A red barrier. Hiding. Like the Capri guy (so he couldn't see the stomach bulge). No steak, spaghetti, even liver. Go fishing. He laughed hard. A cold wind came. It was the Portuguese demonstration. (Tho' I didn't know it at the time.) "Kill all queers," called the crowd. A kid in full flower stood slowly up in a bleeding coffin. Youth Snuffed By Faggot said the sign (In Back Shed). The men marched by in rainbow blouses. Faces covered by bright crosses. They were crying. A singing robin outside woke us up. The sun shining on its breast made it as red as that old convertible Capri.

Smile Babe

We got dressed and went out. A funny demonstration was going by. The men were wrapped in long black robes. A wide space was between each one. They were silent. One stopped and stared. Surprising me as I slid the shiny pennies out of Sister Marilyn's milk bottle. (A beautiful-shaped bottle.) "Let's go," I said to the kid. We got in the car. And started down the driveway. He tried to stop us. I stepped on it and nearly steamrollered him. He pointed at me as we roared off. With a long knife. "Lesbian," he screamed.

We kept moving. In the April field a fist was clutched. (Daffodils from the last feminist demo.) The red spot rose in the rear-view. That old Roxy-red Capri came closer. He had his eye beaded on the short shorts. His body swayed to the rock beat on the radio. The seat rocked.

We stopped at a wool shop. The kid was weaving a lampshade. Bangles, spangles, and white shiny things, to hide the tiny twinkling light. We stopped at the door, seeing someone I sort of knew. "Have to do something about those Portuguese," I said. I don't know why I said that. It was a silly thing to say. "Yeah," she said. "They're after my sister, too." "Who's your sister." "S.," she said. Then I got really scared. S. was the girl with the green eyes.

We got in the car. A cold wind was coming up. Oh thank God it started. You could see the demo way down the street. "I'm-the-quite-empty," I said to the kid. She snuggled closer despite the hole in the floor. Some flowers would be nice. Little sparkling Ps. I could see my lips sinking between the silken velvet petals in search of the strange perfume, of the sunlight flashing like fish beneath the pond's surface. Bright as the teeth of the girl with the green eyes.

The sliding red spot. Smile Babe

We decided to go to the Bargain Basement. To have another look at the Easter Extravaganza. To cheer us up. The glass terrasse was deserted. But the Portuguese were coming. We disappeared down the stairs. There it stood in the Easter sunlight. Purple-rose. Softer than my grandmother's satin slips. I let the petals slide between my fingers. Squeezing slightly. My nose entered the embonpoint. The perfume. I looked over my shoulder. I could see nobody. "Open your schoolbag," I whispered. My mouth was dry. I slipped in the flowers. She smiled. We left quickly.

She was sitting on the back seat holding the flowers. When suddenly the red spot rose up again in the rear-view. Before disappearing in the heavenly blue dust. I put my hand over the visor. When I removed it the red spot was sliding back again. Coming closer and closer. The old Roxy-red Capri. Out of the heavenly blue dust. It entered us from behind. You could see the baby boots on the dashboard. I smiled. The blood ran down my teeth.

The blue-suited security men surrounded my car. The kid was crying on the corrugated ice bank. They flew her to a foreign country. They took me and took my flowers. I was put in a prison by the parking lot. My lips have swollen so, my tongue is like a point in the embonpoint. There's a torn patch in the sky. If only I could smell some F's. Maybe the spring would come back.

bpNICHOL 1944–1988

bpNichol (b. Vancouver, BC) was the creator of the life-long poem, *The Martyrology* (1972–1993). His other major publications included *Journeying & the Returns* (1967), *Konfessions of an Elizabethan Fan Dancer* (1973), *Translating Translating Apollinaire* (1979), *Still* (1983), *Lovev* (1984), *Zygal* (1985), *Art Facts* (1990), and *Truth* (1993). He performed sound-poems in the literary ensemble, The Four Horsemen, and he worked with Steve McCaffery to create a poetic "think tank," the Toronto Research Group. He won the Governor General's Award for his four books of poetry: *Still Water* (1970), *Beach Head* (1970), *The Cosmic Chef* (1970), and *The True Eventual Story of Billy the Kid* (1970). He was renowned for producing beautiful, ephemeral chapbooks.

    Still is the winner of the 3-Day Novel-Writing Contest (a competition in which entrants must compose a lengthy fiction over Labour Day weekend). Just as a *nouveau roman* by Alain Robbe-Grillet might consist of nothing but interminable descriptions so detailed that readers can retain no impression of the setting described, so also does the novel by bpNichol depict in minute detail the scenography for a potential, but postponed, story. Nichol in a interview from 1978 declares: "I've never wanted to describe a landscape. I've wanted to create landscapes"[20] — hence, his words provide a kind of textual terrain across which the eye pans like a camera. He interrupts these acts of description with excerpts from a dialogue between two lovers, whose voices become the soundtrack for these cinematic panoramas.

FROM *STILL*

BY bpNICHOL

FROM the banks of the river, the spray from the rapids making the grass & clay slippery, thru the dark shadows beneath the oaks, the ground worn bare in spots, packed hard from the comings & goings of unnumbered feet, an old footpath makes its way to the edge of the lawn. From the mouth of the river where it loses itself in the larger waters, where the rock & debris strewn shore is daily washed by the movement of the waves, another path winds its way up the bluff face, turns left along the top of the bluff, right along the banks of the river, joining the older footpath as it nears the wood or, if the other direction is taken, losing itself miles later in the long grass that overlooks the vast body of the sea. To walk that way, to look first to the right towards the distant horizon of sea & sky, then left towards the house, makes the house appear as it really is: a small two-storey building to which a front verandah & a back balcony have been added; a farmhouse whose barn has long since disappeared; a house built for a different time & thus a different purpose & place. From the bluffs in a direct line with the little orchard another path winds its way towards the house, bypasses it to loop thru the orchard & then, almost as if continuing the back sidewalk, turns to the right & runs straight out towards the middle of the mountain range. Nearing the beginning of the foothills the path winds & twists, making its way thru ravines & gulleys, old river beds, finding its way to the valleys that run into the heart of the mountains. From those same mountains numerous trails snake out & join to make two main ones: the one that finds its way eventually into the orchard

& a second one that follows the course of the river, joining, finally, the older path that runs towards the house thru the oak wood. The path to the orchard takes three days by foot, & the one that follows the twists & curves of the river six days, sections of the trail continually being obliterated by collapsing river banks until, finally, as the wheat field is reached, the edges of that more precisely defined area can be followed straight across towards the lawn on the left side of the house, the long grass & wheat making passage easy even tho no path exists. From the edge of the lawn, from the point where the old foot-path ends, the white pebbled surface of the winding path that leads to the front door begins. In spring & summer the flowers blooming in the large & small flowerbeds flood the air round the walk with perfume, & the distance from the edge of the lawn to the front verandah is marked by a shifting & blending of fragrance & colour. It is this path & the path from the sea that are favored in these seasons. Returning from the beach in late July thru the long grass at the bluff's edge, or emerging from the dark wood into the bright sun of the lawn, seeing the house, the house appears larger, more imposing, & the curtained windows seem inviting, mysterious, holding forth a promise that is never articulated. In fall the trails to & from the mountains are more frequented, the mud room providing an area in which to remove boots & coats, a place to deposit the sprays of dying leaves, the bits of fossils. As these routes are travelled, the house disappears then reappears as the path dips, turns, moves in behind the hills & rock outcroppings, out again, up, the roof now visible, then the whole building growing larger or smaller depending on the direction travelled. In winter all this is altered, the paths curving around the house & across the lawn from various directions to reach the back door, the front door ignored again until spring. But in the other three seasons of the year unmarked continuations of all these paths, of other paths only temporarily established, criss-cross the lawn toward the front verandah, all of them joining at the foot of the verandah stairs. The coco-matting that covers the stairs is worn &, in places, the staples have worked loose, causing the matting to slide dangerously. The strips covering the porch are worn too & the legs of the couch whose back faces the front railing of the verandah, whose cloth surface is also worn from years of use, first in the livingroom of the house & now, for years, on the front verandah, have worn thru the matting completely & rest on the grey painted floorboards. Only the swinging seat appears new because of the coat of white paint that has been given to it sometime in the past year, sometime in the spring so that the winter snow & frozen air have had no change yet to chip & crack the surface. But the easy chair & the couch, part of the same set purchased when the house was newer, are comfortable & inviting, make sitting on the porch in the warm summer evenings more pleasurable, & the hanging baskets & stone vases give the porch a garden air that the surrounding flower beds accent. Seen from the foot of the verandah stairs, surrounded as they are by the scent of flowers & the distant murmuring of the river, the front door seems less inviting or, more exactly, a thing to be postponed, something to keep closed, sealed, until the moment it is absolutely necessary to use it. As fall turns to winter & the wind from the sea blows in flat across the bluffs, the door is something longed for on returning from skating on the cold ice of the river, longed for precisely because it must remain sealed & the path around the house to the back door seems infinitely long & difficult of access. Running up the path from the river thru the falling rain, reaching the porch, the porch is something to linger on while watching the lightning dance across the sky & strike the distant ground, the front lawn at least three times, the lightning rod on the peak of the house once, & the front door, closed or open, is a source of security, the knowledge that it exists, can be opened, that the house is there & can be entered, reassuring, a presence that embraces by its very familiarity, its nearness &, in reaching for the brass doorknob, turning it, opening the door, a ritual is reenacted whose meaning deepens with each passing year. Pulling the screen door open to turn the handle of the inner door or, the inner door already open or, the screen door not yet in place or already removed & only the one door then to open, crossing the threshold as the door swings inward &, entering the ground floor hallway, turning back to watch the lightning or to close the door quickly because it is winter, because it should not have been opened in the first place no vestibule to absorb the chill air, or leaving it open

because the screen is in place & the house is still hot from the day's accumu-
lations &, standing in the front hallway as the screen door or the front door
swings shut, one enters finally, or for the first time, the inside of the house.
In the diningroom to the left the table has been set. Viewed thru the french
doors the place settings appear, momentarily, as if painted onto the surface of
the oak table, the precise arrangement of the blue cloth napkins, blue china
plates, silver cutlery to either side, & the blue candles in the cut glass can-
dlestick holders (removed from the mantle & placed in the centre of the
table) forming, with the cut glass bowl of white chrysanthemums, a perfect
still life. Thru the leaded windows the back of the easy chair is visible, the
couch, the white pebbled path winding off between the flowerbeds towards
the river. The armchair that had sat in front of the window has been placed
in front of one of the place settings & a number of other diningroom chairs
have been moved from places against the wall & arranged around the table.
The window that looks out on the wheatfield is open & a sliding screen has
been placed in it to both hold it open & keep any straying insects out. From
the fireplace, thru the french doors in the opposite wall, the front door is
visible, the clothes rack, the umbrella stand, the french doors across the hall
&, from the one doorway into the other continuing view of the front lawn is
seen thru each succeeding window, each frame (those in the diningroom, the
leaded ones in the livingroom, the open doorway of the house in between)
recapitulating part of the earlier scene while adding fresh elements to it.
In this way the beginning of the woods is first glimpsed from the diningroom
(a few trees on the left side of the frame), dominates the whole of the open
doorway & then continues to dominate the landscape as seen from the livingroom. A number of magazines lie scattered on the couch to the right as that
room is entered: recent numbers of technical journals devoted to particular
issues in physics & philosophy, a poetry magazine, a copy of a national gossip monthly & copies of various international news weeklies. The books that
were on top of the ladder at the far end of the room have been put away &
a number of new volumes have been removed from the shelves & stacked
on the floor as if the system by which the books had been arranged is now

being reorganized. More volumes are stacked by the easy chairs in front of the fireplace. Along the hall from the front door toward the kitchen nothing has changed. Each painting retains its location, the frames dusted but the arrangement undisturbed, & the letter on the little mail table under the mirror remains unopened & has been joined by a second one. As the door to the kitchen is pushed open, the hinges squeaking as the door swings inward, the hum of the fridge is audible in the hall until the door swings shut again. Here the counter shows signs of food preparation: flour sprinkled on the red top; a cutting board on which a knife rests exactly in the middle of a scattering of small cubes of diced green pepper; a bowl to the right of them containing lettuce, tomatoes, & shredded strips of carrots; in the sink, a number of pots, only their handles visible above the white mound of suds. The preparation table has the largest of the five cutting boards lying in the middle of it & in the middle of the cutting board a roasting chicken has been placed awaiting the toasting of the bread for the stuffing. The chairs around the red table have been pulled back as if in haste & the door to the mud room & the door to the basement are both lying open. From the top of the cellar stairs the basement is too dark to allow any details to be visible & neither the light switch there nor the light switch at the foot of the stairs to the second floor is working. As each of the carpeted steps is climbed, the view that is possible thru the window at the top changes so that first only the sky is visible & then the edge of the bluffs, more & more lawn &, finally, the top stair being reached & the landing stepped onto, the sea beyond all of them. One of the dolls has been removed from the small bedroom & placed in the white wooden chair to the left of the window. The curtains in the small bedroom are drawn, the covers of the bed thrown back, & one of the pillows has fallen off the bed onto the floor & is blocking the door to the closet. The new dolls have been added to the shelves on the right side of the window & the books on the shelves to the left have been rearranged in alphabetical order & stood upright, shiny new blue bookends holding them in place. The mirror in the dresser is tilted so that the back of the top edge is pressing against the wall behind it & the hairline cracks in the painted blue plaster ceiling are reflected. The red carpet in the hall clashes slightly with the blue in the bed-room, more because of the intensity of the pattern than the colour, & here & there has begun to wear thin. In the front bedroom on the left side of the house a suitcase has been thrown on the bed, the contents already taken out & hung behind the closed door of the closet. A dictionary has been borrowed from the bedroom across the hall & placed on the small writing table along with a portable typewriter whose case rests on the floor beside the chair. The window at the front of the house has been thrown open & the fragrances from the various flowerbeds have begun to fill the room & to move thru the open doorway into the hall. The second bedroom is empty. The door to the closet lies open & inside it a number of boxes have been stored, some labelled "books," others labelled "winter clothes," "knickknacks," as if someone were moving or had moved, the process of packing or unpacking not yet finished & the boxes placed here until they could be dealt with. The curtains in the room have been drawn & the light filtering thru them gives the room a quiet, forlorn feeling which the faint perfume of the flowers only intensi-fies. Across the hall the door to the large bedroom lies open, the window facing it looking out over the bluffs & sea, & in the distance, almost at the very horizon, storm clouds are forming, lightning crackling & dancing on the surface of the distant waves, tho on the lawn around the house the sun is still shining & the breeze has not yet shifted in intensity or direction. The cover on the sewing machine in front of the window has been replaced, even tho the basket which has been brought into the room, & now sits to the left of the sewing machine table, contains a number of torn pieces of clothing, & a package of small white buttons has been placed on the right side of the table. A file folder lies open on the desk to the right of the hallway door, the folder's exposed top sheet appearing to be part of a journal or novel, difficult to determine exactly from such a small fragment, to which a number of revisions have been made, the different dates of the revisions hinted at by the shifting colours & shades of ink. A dictionary lies open on the desk to the left of the folder tho the significance of the pages revealed is not immediately apparent since none of the words defined on those particular pages of the dictionary are written on the exposed page of the folder. There are a number of pens lying to the right of the file folder & a small message pad, devoid of writing, in the surface of which the indecipherable indentations made in the course of writing many now non-existent notes appear. Here too the bed is unmade, the pillows having fallen on the floor & a book, a mystery novel, lies open face down on the rumpled sheets. The closet door is open & a number of items of clothing have fallen on the closet floor. The closet light has also been left on. From the hall window at the front the rapids in the river are clearly visible, the white foam of the water as it smashes against the rocks creating tiny whirlpools, easily seen beyond the leafy green branches of the oaks. Down the hall thru the open door of the bathroom, the clothes hamper is visible to the right of the door, is empty when the top is lifted, when the threshold is crossed the top of the clothes hamper is lifted up, placed on the floor, & some article of clothing is or is not dropped into the open basket. The window in the wall opposite the door looks out on the mountains, & the bathtub, wet from recent use, appears as white & cold as the distant peaks. The bathmat is wet & water has pooled on the tiles near the tub & sink. Bits of hair have been caught in both drains & if either set of taps is turned on there is a long wait before hot water comes. The towels which had hung on the wall to the right of the window are now lying in a clump on the floor between the toilet & the end wall. The weights on the scale have been moved, pulling the balancing mechanism down because of the lack of a counter-balance. In the hall the red carpet just outside the door of the bathroom is damp & a number of darker damp spots appear in a semicircle around the larger wet area. Along the hall the door to the upper balcony lies open, the balustrade visible thru the screen door, the orchard beyond, the mountains over which the storm clouds that only a short time ago seemed a safe distance out at sea are now massing. On the inside wall just to the right of the balcony door is the switch which controls the frosted light fixture in the ceiling of the porch and, at night, because of the bug lamp inside it, it casts a muted yellow light. From the hallway of the house looking out onto the balcony a table is visible on the right, two wicker chairs, an ashtray & a deck of cards on the table top &, to the left, thru the thick mesh of the screen door, the porch light not yet on tho the sky is darkening as the storm clouds begin to move closer to the house & the sun to set behind the distant peaks, in the quickening dusk we are aware of two other chairs, another table, & two people who suddenly begin talking.

STEVE MCCAFFERY 1947–

Steve McCaffery (b. Sheffield, England) has performed sound-poems in the literary ensemble The Four Horsemen, and created, with bpNichol, a poetic "think tank," the Toronto Research Group. McCaffery also helped to found the L=A=N=G=U=A=G=E movement, an avant-garde coterie that questions the lyric value of referentiality. His academic works include *North of Intention* (1986) and *Prior to Meaning* (2001), and his literary works include *The Black Debtv* (1989) and *The Cheat of Words* (1996). He has been nominated twice for the Governor General's Award: once for *Theory of Sediment* (1991) and once for *Seven Pages Missing* (2000). He teaches English at York University in Toronto, where he lives with the poet Karen Mac Cormack.

    Panopticon (1984) is an enigmatic whodunnit. Charles Bernstein calls it "the exemplary 'anti-absorptive' book"[21] since it resists the kind of passive reader who might peruse a crime novel for the sake of suspenseful engrossment. The title refers to a mode of surveillance imagined by Jeremy Bentham, who describes a radial prison, built so that cellblocks might encircle a watchtower, where a single, unseen guard can easily observe every inmate. The panopticon symbolizes the maze of words through which the reader must wander, playing the role of invisible spectator, repeatedly viewing the image of a nude woman stepping from her bath. The book replays this scene, like a video or a movie, in which we see ourselves caught in the act of reading about the act of reading itself.

BY STEVE MCCAFFERY

DESCRIPTION of a man (the hero, the killer or the killer's lawyer) replacing a book upon a shelf. Room is probably a study of some kind. Several piles of papers, unsorted index cards, a cold, half-drunk cup of tea. Yellow fragments of typewriter correcting tape. A pencil with a broken tip. The man is not alone. Distant sound of typing fusing with sound of running bath water. A woman's voice. Man sits down at a chair and sorts through the papers spread out before him. The movie ends. Its title: *The Mark*. They leave the cinema and walk east a few blocks towards the phrase "a parked car." As they reach it he notices a small card pushed between the windshield and the wiper blade closest to the driver's side. Distant sound of running water. Mention of a bath. Mention of a place to eat. "Good food at place round the corner" etc. The small card is a parking ticket. He opens the door for her. She says thank you. She gets in. He closes the door. He walks around the front of the car to the other door. He tries to open it but finds it locked. She leans over and pushes up the black plastic peg that locks the car from the inside. Now he can open the door etc. It is possible now to get in etc. Movie end now. Title *Summer Alibi*. He leave cinema alone. She go back study. House very cold. Day called Thursday. The movie ends. Its title is *Panopticon*. She notices that her hands are wet. She dries them on the edge of her jeans. At this point the woman emerges from her bath and commences the ritual of towelling herself dry. She is preparing for an evening at the theatre. Room cold. Tape recorder running. She decides to leave it on and pours herself a drink. Half empty bottle.

* * *

Chapter Seventeen of a book entitled *Panopticon* concludes with a sequence of brief utterances issued by the narrator to a nameless party. The latter has entered a study and replaced a book on a shelf. The book is entitled *Summer Alibi*. In the third brief utterance in this sequence the narrator recalls a similar occasion when she too had entered this same room to replace a letter on a rosewood escritoire. Prior to this entry she had bathed in preparation for an evening at the theatre. It is known (from the evidence of a newspaper advertisement described in detail by the narrator) that the title of the play is *The Mark*. Later, in a book entitled *Panopticon*, this same description will reappear. There, however, the play will be a film and entitled *The Mark* and the whole reference will appear as a cancellarium, printed in an exergual space described as being a cinematic screen in a book the same nameless party has written.

* * *

Start with the assertion that you never failed to locate, nor to execute, any of the following commands. Let the image of the bath persist and split a second time. Place the woman in the room and in the theatre. This time allow the man to walk away. Follow him until you reach the study door. Don't bother to describe the room, just put him in it. Let him meet the other man. Don't mention names. Allow them to leave the room and walk down into the street where a planned complication will occur. Finish the chapter. Switch off the machine. Now place the pen he will use equidistant between the two edges of the page where the two men have been left. Add the phrase "she was middle aged." Now mention another room. Let one of the men go into it. Describe his hands. Describe specifically what the hands are doing. Let the two men walk a block or two before you stop them. Watch them carefully. When you bring them back to the study door make sure the door opens inwards (i.e. away from you) and that the hinged side has a long cracked edge. Now watch how he wipes his hands. Memorize where he puts the book. Note the shelf and the adjacent titles. Note the way he dries his hands and how he refolds the towel. Make sure he notices the cracked edge of the door. Force his eyes to follow the wall until they reach the place where you stand. Don't let him see you. Move away at this point and start to type again. Describe his nose. Describe the marks on his cheek. Make sure there's a new mirror in the bathroom. Make sure you delay him and bring him to the spot too late. Get him anxious. Leave him irritated. Make sure the coffee's cold. Change the time. Set the action in a new place. Change the title. Change the focus of the lens. Turn the lights up to their brightest and shine them directly in his eyes. Repeat the phrase NOTHING NEW WILL OCCUR. Pull back his head by his hair. Keep the curtains closed. Show him the knife. Remove the coffee. Don't let him smoke. Make sure the cup gets broken and that all the coffee spills on the floor. Don't mention the time. Answer all his questions. Bring in a new cup. Now describe the room. Insert four new chairs in the scene you describe. Now change the title to *Toallitas*. Say it's a film. Tell him that you have a part in it. Tell him it's about a murder on board a boat. Then leave him alone in the room. Leave him wondering. Leave the lights on bright. Don't take your eyes off him for a second. Change the title again then move the scene to a different place. Don't let him see where he's going. Place him on a bench in an open park at the east side of the city. Tell him it's spring that's been very sick and now he's recovering. Now switch on the machine and record everything that follows. Use your own voice. Describe the ducks on the pond in the park. Tell him he's going to be all right. Describe the bench he's sitting on. Mention the plaque on it. Mention the words carved into it. Mention the trash can to the side. Now remain silent. Leave quietly. Don't let him know that you're gone. Go back to the study and watch the other man. Ask him all the questions you can think of that might relate to his movements over the past five days. Sit him in a chair with a high back. Focus the bright light on his eyes. Finish the sentence then let him move to the door. Force him to take up the pen and write some more.

Tell the other man that he's a woman. If he tries to shift the scene or mentions the strategic sections of the woman emerging delete him from your own story. Describe him in such a way that he'll be dead. Put parentheses around the whole incident and leave quietly. Replace the entire paragraph with the phrase HIS BODY REMAINED MOTIONLESS AND A COLD LUMP CAME IN HER THROAT. If he writes he's dead then shift the scene to the garden and replace the former line with the phrase HE'S MOVING QUIETLY TOWARDS THE GATE. Now you can drop the spoon. Don't tell either of them about the contents of the letter. Finish it off with a brief history of the place. Polish off the room in a brief sentence. Describe the woman getting out of the bath. Change the title of the book to *The Mind of Pauline Brain*. Now watch carefully how the keys drop to his feet between his shoes. Don't describe them. Look very carefully at his face. Now watch him pick up the spoon. Make him put it on the escritoire. Now make him pick up the key. Introduce a sudden noise that frightens him. Let him run to the door but make sure the door's locked. Tell him a lie. Tell him you've just returned from a visit to a friend. Lie and say you've forgot the name. Don't mention the movie. Stop the sentence just as he's about to leave. Repeat the phrase I BELIEVE THE DOOR IS ALWAYS KEPT LOCKED. At this point the other man might ask you where the keys are. Tell him you've lost them. Make sure you freeze him and describe him in detail (facial features, mannerisms, family background etc.) Describe your own return to the park. Now interrupt as many conversations as you can. Make sure that he's watching you as you watch him. In the book describe him as a woman. It's important to keep control of this surveillance scenario as long as you possibly can. Don't worry that you can't see, make sure, however, that when you can't see that somebody else can. Now you can delete all reference to the spoon. Repeat the phrase NOTHING NEW WILL OCCUR. Now delete the second man. Remove the eighth, the sixteenth and the thirty ninth paragraphs. Return them to their files in the desk. Now take out the index file and check the possible descriptions. Pause from your typing to look at the man in the park. Switch off the taperecorder. Check that all books are back on the shelf. Now let him close his eyes. Let him get up from the bench and open them again. Let him walk towards you. Switch the scene suddenly to a year ago in the study. Take off the blindfold. Make him turn on the switch. Describe him in a position of abject terror. Tell him it's all right. Make him walk across the floor to the window. Describe him looking out. Replace the blindfold as he reaches the final sentence. Describe him as writing rather than reading. Change the final sentence to something else. Make sure you keep it vague and ambiguous. Leave the body in the room. Now describe whatever you want. When you leave the room make sure the machine is switched off, the book is replaced on the shelf, that the light is out and the door locked. Check your watch as you leave. It should be precisely nine thirty seven.

* * *

It is a rule of the specific game (the one called "the movie" in the book entitled *The Mark*) that a change in character occur only at a point when the feasibility of plot itself seems dead. A woman, for instance, who emerges from a bath to find the hero (not the killer) standing by her with a knife. A photograph of the knife might show butter on the blade. Butter purchased three days ago from a small delicatessen owned by a distant relative of the nameless woman. In Chapter Seventeen of a book entitled *Summer Alibi* this shop is described in great detail. Its external features enumerated and the interior rooms and content therein elaborately itemized. It is mentioned too that each day the shop closes at six. It is closed all day Sunday. The book describes a hand which, a few seconds before or after six, reaches down to the glass plate door and reverses a hanging sign. At nine thirty-seven in the morning the sign reads *Open*. The narrator of *Summer Alibi* imputes great significance to this action and describes an incident of considerable violence occurring one day when a woman entered the shop to purchase a bottle of shampoo to be used later in her evening shower. The title of the movie in which this entire game scenario is enacted is *The Mind of Pauline Brain*. It is understandable how, at this point of impasse, in both book and movie a certain predictability obtrudes. Once again the camera shows a woman emerging from a bath, towelling herself dry and remembering the incident of the shop. There are red marks on her body to suggest an earlier scene of violence. Let us call this obsession caused by impasse the "conscious de-idealization of the performing properties." The entire movie has now emerged as a misconception, a philosophical mistake on the director's part. The movie is proving to be a major political mistake, the victim (if you like) of a fake historical decision. During actual production many scenes will be cut. It must be imagined that this is how the story of the lady vanishes. Let us assume that technicians are currently at work trying to retrieve a specific sequence of shots that show a camera held in front of a half concealed rose-wood escritoire. The film has apparently snapped causing the loss of a certain number of valuable frames. It is a hot day. The escritoire was bought espe-cially for the scene from a small antique store in the village owned by the producer's niece (a part-time writer). Both niece and producer seem embar-rassed. She averts her face. He has apparently put some question to her which she has no mind to answer. Voice at her elbow. The screen becomes blank. In the dark of the theatre only the neon exit signs are perceptible. It is rain-ing outside and the camera focuses upon two solitary walking people in the street. To their left (but at a distance of several blocks) there is a large illuminated theatre sign. The verbal contents of the sign are in the process of being changed to announce the forthcoming attraction. It is to be a film about analogy and presence, a film based on the game of chess in which all the pieces must be removed from a box for a certain biography to continue.

* * *

Chapter Twenty Six of a book entitled *The Mind of Pauline Brain* ends with a sequence of brief utterances spoken by the hero to a nameless woman. The woman has previously been described as having retired to her bath after a short visit to her study where she replaced a book upon a shelf. The title of this book is *Panopticon*. Previous to this description it was stated that the woman was alone and reading a letter received that morning. During her reading of this letter her mind is described as wandering among a confused memory of the film she had seen three nights ago. In the film is a scene in which a nameless photographer is described as having died. The actual incident is not portrayed but through a sequence of brief utterances a strong suggestion is left that the photographer's death was a very violent one. The title of the film is *The Mark*. In a brief and critical review of the film published in that morning's paper it is mentioned that the filmscript is based on a book entitled *Summer Alibi* and that in chapter thirty three of that book occurs the incident of a woman reading. It is there that the woman is described as emerging from a bath, towelling herself dry and reaching over to a book upon a shelf. Naked and half dry she reads the spine: *Toallitas*. Despite the title she remembers the book as containing little or no Spanish. She can't reconstitute the plot except for vague and broken memories with little or no connexion. Should this memory itself be rendered writing it would take the form of a long, extended strip or horizontal band along the bottom of several blank pages. This writing, naturally, she would never find possible to read. It would occur, in effect, as a lineal band of prohibition, a fictive threshold, an exergual space outside her own sphere of existence but within the compass of an authentic reader's eyes. As if the reader's book alone contained the possibility of that other story. It would be as if the woman had arrived late and in confusion at a movie. The film already started. The title unknown to her. She sees the image of a man which finally captures her attention. But the screen is entirely vacant. It seems again "as if" the reel of film has snapped and the movie is temporarily interrupted. Whatever the reason when the image finally returns the entire body of the man is no longer in evidence. Now there is the close up of small hand camera held in front of a face. The image is blurred and granular and might be compared to the stereophonic text of a voice recorded in the worst possible acoustic conditions and in a language the woman cannot understand. To the trained reader's eyes this might be rendered as a horizontal band dividing two areas of discourse extended out across the top and bottom of page. Previous to the band's appearance several pages of the text are presumed to have occurred with no such division. The band, it is assumed, has snapped and only at this point repaired. Suffice it to say that even with the band reconnected there is no point of contact in the several threads of discourse. The film, the book and the tape are said to be hermetic and sealed within the vacuum of a vacant space. There are no proper names to imbricate or link. No reference across the technologic spaces. No calling. No touch or utterance. No sudden bump. As such, two people might pass along a street. But there can be no town. No lights. No rooms to be among. There are two separated and entirely differentiated passages and no specified direction. The possibility of loss has been removed.

AFTERWORD

AVANT-GARDE fiction in Canada has never enjoyed much cultural prestige, largely because such fiction has often called into question the pragmatic, if not parochial, values of cultural identity still dominant in much of our realist fiction. Canada has never deigned to support a world-class, avant-garde movement, despite the innovative traditions found in other countries. While Canada has existed as a nation for as long as the avant-garde itself, only a smattering of unorthodox books grace the canon before 1965 (for example, *The Double Hook*, by Sheila Watson, and *By Grand Central Station I Sat Down and Wept*, by Elizabeth Smart). After 1965, during the cultural outburst of the Centennial, we see a new generation of writers begin to test the limits of narrative potential, but since the early 1980s, this effusive activity has diminished without coalescing into a coherent tradition of anti-classic, anti-mimetic writing. While the *écriture automatique* of André Breton, the *nouveau roman* of Alain Robbe-Grillet, or the *écriture féminine* of Hélène Cixous may still continue to influence the work of many Québecois novelists, such European writers from the radical fringes of modernism have had a far less sustained influence upon the work of Canadian novelists situated elsewhere in the country.

Linda Hutcheon has argued that, nevertheless, Canada remains rich in unorthodox, postmodern literature, but ironically, to make such a case, she has had to locate its anti-classic, anti-mimetic agenda in realist writing.[22] While Hutcheon argues that postmodern literature occupies a marginal position at the periphery of culture, she does not discuss such fiction on the grounds that it has only a minor status among the major voices in Canada. Often critics evade any encounter at all with the truly scary avant-garde, ignoring the rare cases of a more experimental genre in order to depict as progressive the many cases of a more conservative genre. Only a few writers of anti-classic, anti-mimetic fiction have ever produced an avant-garde oeuvre of consistent quality according to a consistent mandate throughout an entire career. With a few noteworthy exceptions, most writers of avant-garde literature in this country have dabbled in such work and then have either modulated or abandoned their commitment to it for any number of reasons: decades of critical reproach, demands of economic exigency, rewards of ordinary practice, changes in literary interest, etc.

Margaret Atwood has seen fit, however, to redress such neglect by suggesting that House of Anansi Press republish some of the most interesting, but often disregarded, examples of avant-garde English fiction in Canada. While other contemporary anthologies, such as *Likely Stories* (edited by Linda Hutcheon and George Bowering), may feel obliged to make compromises in their choices, relying heavily upon selections of unusual, realist fiction by canonic authors in order to accommodate the generic demands for digestible literature, *Ground Works* makes no such concessions, preferring instead to offer the best work from the most provocative experiments yet performed by the broadest spectrum of writers in the country. This anthology does not pretend to represent a particular aesthetic viewpoint, nor does it attempt to distinguish between practising modernists and their postmodern successors. The literati included here do not constitute a coherent movement of consistently experimental writers whose entire oeuvre brims with innovative iconoclasm. On the contrary, these works constitute a brief encyclopedia of millenary potential, whose possibilities still await further exploration and further development by a subsequent generation of storytellers.

Contributors to *Ground Works* represent a diverse variety of revolutionary sensibilities, ranging from late eighteenth-century excesses (as exemplified by Chris Scott) to late twentieth-century excesses (as exemplified by Leonard Cohen). Audrey Thomas and Graeme Gibson convey the psychology of their characters through the use of stream-of-consciousness, while Ray Smith and Matt Cohen renounce all psychological prerequisites for such characterization. Gail Scott and J. Michael Yates write stories in a manner reminiscent of *les écrivains surréalistes*, while the works of bpNichol and Steve McCaffery recall the fiction of *les nouveaux romanciers*. Andreas Schroeder, Derk Wynand, and Robert Zend all respond directly to the magic realism of surreal writers from Europe, while other contributors find inspiration in avant-garde writers from America: George Bowering responding to Gertrude Stein; Daphne Marlatt responding to Charles Olson; Christopher Dewdney responding to William S. Burroughs. Some contributors even emulate the non-academic, non-literary media of popular culture, taking cues from either comic books (as do Michael Ondaatje and John Riddell) or genre films (as do David Godfrey and Martin Vaughn-James).

Contributors to this anthology pursue eclectic, literary interests, experimenting with many varieties of radical fiction in an effort to find a genre appropriate to the sociocultural circumstances of Canada. While the stories here constitute some of the most adventurous fiction yet written in this country, much of it has, nevertheless, languished in obscurity, doing more perhaps to inspire the next wave of avant-garde poetlings than to inspire the next wave of avant-garde novelists. While the classic, mimetic novel may still dominate the modern milieu of literature, such realist fiction often does so at the expense of indigenous innovation. Many avant-garde writers must contend with tepid support from a community of indifferent, if not uninitiated, peers, many of whom might dismiss experimentation as nothing more than an excuse for lousy prose. The American novelist Brion Gysin has averred that writing lags at least fifty years behind painting,[23] and his comments about the philistine sensibility of literature apply all the more aptly to Canada at the very moment when our writers have begun to receive unprecedented international acclaim. The work in this anthology, however, reminds us that to explore the limits of language, literature must often put its own most elementary principles at risk.

— CHRISTIAN BÖK, TORONTO, MARCH 2002

NOTES

1   See *Canadian Novelists and the Novel*. Ed. Douglas Raymond and Leslie Monkman. Borealis: Ottawa, 1981. Or contact Canadian Centre for Studies in Publishing.

2   Hutcheon, Linda. *The Canadian Postmodern: A Study of Contemporary English-Canadian Fiction*. Toronto: Oxford University Press, 1988. 27.

3   Thomas, Audrey. "An Interview with Audrey Thomas." With Eleanor Wachtel. *A Room of One's Own*. 10:3–4 (March 1986): 7–61. 43.

4   Nicholson, Colin. "Of Oracles and Orreries: Graeme Gibson and his Writing." *British Journal of Canadian Studies* 3:2 (1988): 293–307. 297.

5   Smith, Ray. "Author's Commentary." *Sixteen by Twelve: Short Stories by Canadian Writers*. Ed. John Metcalf. Toronto: Ryerson, 1970. 219–224. 220, 224.

6   Scobie, Stephen. "Two Authors in Search of a Character." *Canadian Literature* 54 (Autumn 1972): 37–55. 44.

7   New, W. H. "Artifice and Experience." *Canadian Literature* 53 (Summer 1972): 88–94. 92.

8   Yates, J. Michael. "During." http://www.alsopreview.com/yates/writing/during.html.

9   Bowering, George. "Andreas Schroeder." In *Fiction of Contemporary Canada*. Toronto: Coach House, 1980. 16.

10 Dewdney, Christopher. "Parasite Maintenance." *Open Letter* 4.6/7 (Winter 1980–1981). 19–35. 20.

11 Cohen, Matt. "Notes on Realism in Modern English-Canadian Fiction." In *Canadian Writers in 1984: 25th Anniversary Issue of Canadian Literature*. Ed. W. H. New. Vancouver: University of British Columbia Press, 1984. 65–71.

12 Vaughn-James, Martin. "A Statement." *Canadian Fiction Magazine* 42 (1982): 20–25. 21.

13 Bowering, George. "The Three-Sided Room: Notes on the Limitations of Modernist Realism." In *The Mask in Place: Essays on Fiction in North America*. Winnipeg: Turnstone Press, 1982. 19–31. 20.

14 Marlatt, Daphne. "Preface." In *Ghost Works*. Edmonton: NeWest Press, 1993. vii–viii.

15 Wershler-Henry, Darren. "[Concatenation Hemorrhaging [Framing [John Riddell]]. *Open Letter* 8.8 (Winter 1994): 115–127. 125.

16 Davey, Frank. "Dave Godfrey." In *From There to Here*. Erin: Press Porcépic, 1974. 126–128. 127.

17   Cain, Stephen. "Play's the Thing: The Visual Poetry of Robert Zend." *Open Letter* 10.6 (Summer 1999): 50–61. 52.

18   Abley, Mark. "Poets in Prose." *Canadian Literature* 92 (Spring 1982): 76–77. 76.

19   Scott, Gail. "Shaping a Vehicle for Her Use." In *Spaces Like Stairs*. Toronto: The Women's Press, 1989. 65–76. 68.

20   Nichol, bp. "bpNichol." With Caroline Bayard and Jack David. In *Out-posts/Avant-Postes*. Erin: Press Porcépic, 1978. 15–49. 32.

21   Bernstein, Charles. "Panoptical Artifice." *Open Letter* 6.9 (Fall 1987): 9–15. 13.

22   Hutcheon, Linda. *The Canadian Postmodern: A Study of Contemporary English-Canadian Fiction*. Toronto: Oxford University Press, 1988. 20.

23   Gysin, Brion. "Cut-Ups Self-Explained." In *The Third Mind* by William S. Burroughs and Brion Gysin. New York: Viking Press, 1978. 34–37. 34.

ACKNOWLEDGEMENTS

"Book Three: Beautiful Losers" from *Beautiful Losers* (New York: Viking Press, 1966) by Leonard Cohen. Copyright © 1966 by Leonard Cohen. Used by permission, McClelland & Stewart Ltd.

"If One Green Bottle . . ." from *Ten Green Bottles* (New York: Bobbs Merrill, 1967) by Audrey Callahan Thomas. Copyright © 1967 by Audrey Callahan Thomas. Used by permission of the author. This story was originally published in *The Atlantic Monthly*, June 1965.

Excerpt from *Five Legs* (Toronto: House of Anansi Press, 1969) by Graeme Gibson. Copyright ©1969, Graeme Gibson. Used by permission of the author.

"Raphael Anachronic" from *Cape Breton Is the Thought-Control Centre of Canada* (Toronto: House of Anansi Press, 1969) by Ray Smith. Copyright © 1969, 1989, 2002. Used by permission of the author.

"Billy the Kid and the Princess" from *The Collected Works of Billy the Kid* (Toronto: House of Anansi Press, 1970) by Michael Ondaatje. Reprinted by permission of Ellen Levine Literary Agency, Inc. Copyright ©1970 by Michael Ondaatje.

Chapter One from *Bartleby* (Toronto: House of Anansi Press, 1971) by Chris Scott. Copyright © Chris Scott, 1971. Used by permission of the author.

"And Two Percent Zero" from *The Abstract Beast* (Victoria: Sono Nis Press, 1971) by J. Michael Yates. Copyright © 1971 by J. Michael Yates. Reprinted by permission of J. Michael Yates.

"The Connection" from *The Late Man* (Victoria: Sono Nis Press, 1972) by Andreas Schroeder. Copyright © 1972 by Andreas Schroeder. Used by permission of the author. "The Connection" has also appeared in the fiction anthology *Sunlight & Shadows* (Toronto: Thomas Nelson & Sons, 1974) and in the English literature textbook *Inquiry into Literature, Vol.* 3 (Toronto: Collier MacMillan, 1980).

"Remote Control" from *Fovea Centralis* (Toronto: Coach House Books, 1975) by Christopher Dewdney. Copyright © 1975 by Christopher Dewdney. Used by permission of the author.